By ETHEL CALVERT PHILLIPS

First published in 1937

www.thegoodandthebeautiful.com

Cover illustration by Larissa Sharina

and Maginel Wright Barney

Inside illustrations by Maginel Wright Barney

Cover design by Phillip Colhouer

Round and round and round he turned in a dance. *(page 27)*

Table of Contents

CHAPTER 1
CALICO

There was a new pony at Rocky Farm.

His name was Calico. This must have been because he was a calico pony, spotted black and white.

He was a pretty pony. His coat was the blackest black and the whitest white that you could hope to see. He had four white stockings and a white star on his forehead too. His ears were perky, his tail was long and thick, and his eyes were brown and bright and full of fun.

Calico had come riding on a train to Rocky Farm. He traveled in a great wooden crate with his head just looking over the edge. He had been sent from a ranch out West that was miles and miles and miles away from Rocky Farm.

Calico had not always lived at the ranch.

Where had he been before that? Well, of course Calico couldn't tell. If he had been able to talk, everyone would have listened with surprise and delight to what he had to say. You may be sure of that.

When he finished, they would have begged him to tell more and more.

At any rate, there he was at the ranch. But he had been there such a short time that the only person he knew was a cowboy named Jim.

Jim took care of Calico. He wore a bright handkerchief knotted around his neck, a pair of high-heeled riding boots, and a large cowboy hat.

There were so many horses and ponies and cowboys on the ranch that Calico could hardly tell one from another. And before he had time to feel at home, off he started on his long journey to Rocky Farm.

Jim told him where he was going.

"You have been sold, Calico," said Jim, rubbing Calico's nose with a friendly hand. "A farmer in the East, in the State of Vermont, wants a pony just like you."

So one morning Calico, in the big wooden crate, found himself on the platform of the railway station. His name, "Calico," was painted in great black letters on the side of the box.

Calico peered over the edge of his crate. It all seemed very strange to the little pony. He stamped his foot. He opened his mouth to neigh.

But just then there came a rattle and a roar, and around the curve swept the train. Calico was lifted on board. With a puff and a hoot and a whistle the train started. Off rode Calico on what was to be a very long journey indeed.

The train bumped and swayed and rattled on its way. Up the hills, around the curves, and down into the valleys it sped. It stopped at the stations with a jerk and a shrill whistle. Then with a puff-f-f! and a hoot, toot, toot! it was off again. On and on and on went the train.

At last the journey came to an end. When Calico, in his crate, was lifted out, he was a stiff and tired little pony, as you may guess.

But there at the railroad station, a pleasant man in blue overalls was waiting for him. That was Farmer Drake. A little boy with a freckled nose was hopping up and down at sight of the pony. That was Billy, Farmer Drake's grandson. "Harum-scarum Billy" he was sometimes called. That will tell you what kind of a little boy Billy was. He didn't live at the farm. He came visiting now and then.

"He is my pony! His name is Calico! He is my pony!" called Billy, jumping until the dust flew.

Carefully, Calico was taken from the crate. Then Farmer Drake and Billy led Calico home. Slowly, they climbed the steep mountain roads until at last the big stable at Rocky Farm was reached. Tired Calico was glad of a good supper and a warm bed of soft hay.

A long night's rest was what Calico needed. In the morning he felt like a different pony. He was as lively and frisky as he could be.

How pleasant it was at Rocky Farm! How many, many ponies lived there too! Wherever Calico looked, he saw a pony. They were every color: gray and chestnut, black and sorrel, white and bay.

The pasture meadow was dotted with ponies. Some of them were galloping round and round in a circle, head tossing, tail flying. Others shrilled and whinnied with pleasure as they dashed up the hillside in a frolic. Here was a pony peacefully cropping the sweet green grass. There lay a plump fellow down on his back taking a pony roll. He scrubbed himself to and fro. His tail flopped. His four little legs waved in the air.

There was a good reason for so many ponies. This

was a pony farm. Farmer Drake raised ponies and sold them. Sometimes he hired them out to people too.

Billy had visited his grandfather so often that he knew all about ponies. Now what good times he and Calico had! They ran and raced and romped in the meadow. Billy went riding on Calico too.

For four happy days, they played together. Then Billy had to go home.

It was hard to say goodbye to Calico. Billy put both arms about the pony's neck and held him close.

"I like you best of all the ponies," said Billy. "I will come back and ride you again. You see if I don't."

Then Billy was gone and Calico stood in the meadow, looking over the stone wall at the brook.

It was a swift little brook. It rushed and foamed and tumbled over the stones and pebbles. Merrily it hurried on its way down the mountain, singing a cheerful song.

Calico stood for a long time watching the brook. He seemed to be thinking. His ears twitched. Slowly, he swished his long tail.

What could the little pony be thinking?

It might be he was saying to himself, "Everyone is going somewhere. Billy has gone, and the brook is hurrying off too."

Suddenly Calico tossed his head. He stamped his little hoof. He looked so full of mischief that it was easy to guess his thoughts.

"Ho!" perhaps Calico was thinking, "why can't I run away too?"

CHAPTER 2
AN EXCITING DAY

It was a bright, warm summer morning, and Roxy was ready for a busy day.

The sun looked in at the kitchen window. He saw that breakfast was over. He saw a little girl drying dishes. She was helping her mother, and she was talking very fast as she worked.

"First, I will take Poky down to the pasture, Mother," the little girl was saying, "and then I will feed the chickens. Perhaps Father will take me riding with him today. He is going to see about building a man's new barn."

Roxy was a thin, quick little girl with hazel-brown eyes and short brown hair that curled all over her head. She looked like her mother, so everyone said.

She was a little country girl. She lived with her father and mother in a plain white house that stood at the foot of a mountain. The mountain was called "Old Moody" after a man who had once lived at the very tip-top. It was halfway up Old Moody that Farmer

Drake had his pony farm. And past the side of Roxy's house ran the noisy, hurrying little mountain brook.

There were only six houses, counting Roxy's, built there at the foot of Old Moody. There wasn't a single store nor a church nor a school. But the tiny hamlet had a name, a droll name. It was called Little Turkey. Roxy knew everyone who lived in the five other houses of Little Turkey, and they all knew Roxy too.

Roxy's father, Mr. Hatfield, was a carpenter. He was a tall man and very strong, as a carpenter should be. His shop was only a stone's throw away from his house. Roxy and her mother could hear the "z-z-z-z!" of his saw and the "rap-tap-tap!" of his hammer whenever he was there at work.

At last, the breakfast dishes were dried and put away in the cupboard.

"Now I will take Poky to pasture," said Roxy. "I hope the chickens aren't hungry. They will just have to wait."

The big red barn stood back of the house, and in the barn lived Poky and Mrs. Jingle.

Poky was a cow, a gentle, fawn-colored Jersey cow. She was called Poky because she moved so slowly. She couldn't have had a better name.

Mrs. Jingle was the automobile that carried Roxy and her father and mother over the steep and stony country roads. The sturdy little car climbed the hills and dipped into the valleys with a rattling and a creaking and a jingling that gave it its name.

Down the road went Poky with Roxy at her heels. Watch, the yellow collie dog, bounded on ahead.

"There is no use telling you to hurry, I suppose," said Roxy as Poky ambled slowly along. "But remember that the hens haven't had a bite of breakfast. You had yours hours ago, you know."

Poky's bell jangled softly. Neatly she nipped off a red clover blossom growing by the side of the road. Then she really seemed to walk a little faster. Perhaps she felt sorry for the hungry hens.

At any rate, it wasn't long before Roxy and Watch came running back along the road, leaving Poky safe in the pasture.

Then off went Watch to look at a chipmunk's hole that he had his eye on, and Roxy gave the hens their breakfast. She scattered the corn with a generous hand.

"Careful, Claribel, careful," warned Roxy, as she saw a hungry hen rudely push her neighbor aside.

Claribel was Roxy's own little brown hen. Her feathers grew the wrong way and this gave her a surprised, excited look.

"How in the world am I going to teach you manners, Claribel?" went on Roxy. "Don't you want to be polite?"

Claribel shook her tail feathers in answer and snapped up the largest grain of corn in sight. So, with a sigh for Claribel's rudeness, Roxy climbed the stairs into the barn loft to look for eggs.

It was pleasant in the loft, packed with sweet-smelling hay. A dusty sunbeam stole through a crack and turned a great lacy cobweb to silver. The barn swallows skimmed past the window. A brisk little breeze went rustling by. Roxy, hunting in the hay, found three white eggs.

In the buttery, a small, cool room off the kitchen, Roxy left the new eggs. It was then that she heard a sound coming down the road. It was a quick, lively, lippety-clippety sound.

Roxy ran to the front gate. Nearer and nearer came the noise. Louder and louder it grew.

Roxy laughed out loud when she saw what was

making the noise.

It was a little black and white pony!

He came galloping along, his head in the air. His tail flew out behind him. His mane blew in the wind. There was a merry air about him, as if he were out for fun. He wore neither saddle nor bridle. On he came, as free and as swift as the summer breeze.

"I believe he is running away," thought Roxy.

And she was quite right.

Of course it was Calico, runaway, mischievous Calico, who had jumped the stone wall and splashed in the brook and started down the mountain as fast as he could pelt.

But Roxy knew nothing of all this. She only knew that here was the prettiest black and white pony that she had ever seen.

"Here, pony! Here, pony!" called Roxy, as Calico reached the front gate.

Very much to Roxy's surprise, the pony stood still.

Then he did the strangest thing. Roxy couldn't believe her eyes. But it did happen. She saw it. She knew it was true.

The pony stood on his hind legs and turned round and round and round. It was almost as if he were dancing, Roxy thought.

Then down he came on all fours and looked at Roxy in the friendliest way.

"How did you like it?" his look seemed to say.

Roxy laughed and clapped her hands.

"Do it again, pony," she called. "Do it again."

But the pony tossed his head, and off he galloped, lippety-clippety, up the road.

"Oh! He has gone!" exclaimed Roxy, disappointed. "I wish he had stayed."

But the pony hadn't gone. No, indeed, he hadn't. Back he came at a smart pace, and Roxy saw that he was galloping, not on four legs, but on three! His fourth leg stood out stiff and straight before him.

"I never knew such a pony," said Roxy in delight. "What are you going to do next?"

The next thing the pony did was to stand on his hind legs again. Now he was walking on them, walking backwards, too!

This was too wonderful. Someone else must come and see.

"Mother! Mother!" called Roxy. "Father! Come see the pony! Do!"

But by the time Mr. Hatfield stepped out of his shop, the pony was down on his four little feet again. When Mrs. Hatfield came hurrying around the house, he was only sniffing Roxy's hand with a soft and friendly nose.

"He isn't like other ponies," explained Roxy, so excited that she couldn't talk fast enough. "He can dance, and run on three legs, and walk on two feet."

"Can he do all that? He is a wonderful pony!" said Mr. Hatfield with a laugh. "Show us your tricks, pony."

But the pony only nibbled the grass by the roadside and swished his tail. Not in any way did he show Roxy's father and mother what a wonderful pony he was.

"You must be mistaken, Roxy," said Mrs. Hatfield. "You must have imagined it all."

At this, Roxy shook her head. She knew that it had happened. She knew very well that she had not made a mistake.

"Here comes Farmer Drake, riding fast," said Roxy's father, looking up the road. "This is probably one of his ponies. He can tell us whether the pony can do the tricks that Roxy thinks she saw."

Farmer Drake only laughed at the question.

"He is a new pony," said the farmer, "and I haven't seen any tricks yet. His name is Calico, and he is full of mischief. He has run away from his pasture. Come, Runaway, come home."

With a halter around his neck, Calico, stepping lightly, was led away.

But he looked back once at Roxy with a mischievous roll of the eye. His ears twitched in a knowing fashion, and he gave a soft whinny that was almost a laugh.

"Of course he did the tricks. He is telling me so," cried Roxy.

She laughed delightedly as she watched the pony prance out of sight.

Roxy talked about Calico at dinner. She talked of

him again when she went riding that afternoon with her father in Mrs. Jingle.

That night after supper Roxy sat on the doorstep. Watch was keeping her company. The crickets were playing their shrill little fiddles. The brown brook was singing a quiet evening song.

"I do hope I see that pony again," Roxy was thinking.

In the deep blue sky, out shone a bright star, and Roxy made a wish on it.

"I can't tell you my wish, Watch," said Roxy to the big yellow dog at her side, "or it won't come true. But it is about something with four legs and a long tail and his name begins with C."

CHAPTER 3

WHAT THE MAILMAN BROUGHT

The next morning Roxy woke early. The telephone was ringing, and Roxy could hear her father answering it.

"Come, Roxana, it is a telegram for you," Mr. Hatfield was saying.

Roxana, of course, was Roxy's mother.

Roxy hurried downstairs in her nightgown. She couldn't wait to hear what the telegram said.

"It is from little Oliver Pope's father," Mrs. Hatfield told Roxy. "He has telegraphed to ask whether Oliver may spend the summer with us here."

"Oliver is the little boy who lives in New York and hasn't any mother, isn't he?" asked Roxy. "I know about him. You went to school with his mother when you were little girls, and we are friends with his father. Are you going to let him come?"

"Of course, I want him to come," answered Roxy's mother. "Father is telephoning a telegram now."

"What did your telegram say?" asked Roxy. "Read

MAGINEL WRIGHT BARNEY

me just what it said."

So Mrs. Hatfield read the telegram: "'May Oliver spend summer with you stop telegraph reply stop see letter.'"

"See letter," repeated Roxy slowly. "That means that a letter is coming. Perhaps it will come today. I must watch for Beely. I do hope he won't be late."

Beely was the mailman. He drove past Roxy's house every day and left the mail. He put it in a box that stood on a post beside the front gate. The box had Roxy's name—Hatfield—painted on it, and it glittered like silver in the sun.

Beely was busy all day long traveling over the country roads and leaving mail in shining little boxes all along the way. In summer, he rode in an automobile. In winter, he drove a horse and sleigh.

Beely and Roxy were old friends. Indeed, Beely was Roxy's next door neighbor. His house stood on the other side of a cornfield down the road.

Beely lived all alone in the brightest house in Little Turkey. You would have to go far and wide to find a house as bright as his. It was painted half a dozen different colors. Beely's brother, who lived on the other side of the mountain, was a painter. And he gave Beely all his odds and ends of leftover paint.

Roxy thought that Beely's house was beautiful.

"I like it much better than our white house," she often said. "We have only green shutters and a green front door."

Roxy could tell you all the colors on Beely's house.

"The front is yellow," she would say, naming them on her fingers, "and one side is blue. The other side is white, and the back is chocolate brown. The door is blue, and the roof is green, and the chimney is bright red. I wish I lived in that kind of a house."

Roxy often watched at the gate for Beely to drive by, and today she meant to be there without fail.

She ate her breakfast in such a hurry that her mother had to speak to her twice. When she dried the dishes, she rattled the cups and saucers and flourished the plates until it seemed as if there must be a crash.

Poky ambled so slowly down the road to pasture that Roxy almost thought she would have to find a switch. As for the hens, they were whisked through their morning meal at a pace that must have made their little heads spin.

Watch, his golden eyes bright, seemed to know that there was something exciting in the air. He whirled round and round after his own tail and then dashed off to worry the plump chipmunk who lived so snugly under the stone wall.

Roxy was now upstairs helping her mother. The spare room must be made ready for Oliver. Roxy waved a large duster as she busily worked and talked.

"Oliver will like Poky and Watch and the brook, Mother. Don't you think he will?" asked Roxy. "I am glad he is coming. I can hardly wait."

Soon she heard the sound of an automobile.

"There is Beely," she cried. "He has come with the letter."

Downstairs she ran, as fast as a little girl can go.

No, it was not Beely.

But what a strange sight met her eyes!

It was a small house on wheels fastened behind an automobile. A trailer, to be sure! Roxy had never before seen one close by. The mountain roads were too steep and narrow for many trailers to come that way.

The little house and the car were at a standstill in the road not far from Roxy's door. A man and a woman were filling bottles with water from the brook.

Roxy could see inside the trailer. There were bunks against the wall for beds. There was a folding shelf for a table. A small cupboard was filled with blue dishes. There was even a bit of carpet on the floor.

"See the chimney on the roof!" exclaimed Roxy, speaking out loud in her surprise. "Yes, there is a little stove inside. I could bake custards, the kind I make for Father, if anybody asked me to go along."

She was staring so earnestly at the checked curtains in the tiny windows that she did not hear the honk of Beely's horn. Off moved the trailer, and Roxy turned around to see Mailman Beely, ruddy and white-haired, laughing at her from his usual seat.

But there was no letter in Beely's hand.

For a moment, Roxy felt disappointed. Then she looked again and began to understand why Beely laughed.

On the seat beside him sat a little boy. He was not one of the country children. He was a stranger. Roxy had never seen him before.

But she knew in a moment who it was, and she said so at once.

“It is Oliver!” exclaimed Roxy. “I know it is. But where is the letter? The telegram said, ‘See letter,’ and Oliver has come instead.”

At the sound of his name, the little boy smiled at Roxy. He had been looking rather shy and sober before. It was a friendly smile. It made Roxy feel that Oliver would be a pleasant visitor and good fun.

Oliver’s eyes were as blue as cornflowers. His yellow hair was straight under his dark blue cap. He was a city boy, it was plain to be seen. His cheeks were not rosy, like Roxy’s. Roxy looked down at the scratches on her brown fingers. Oliver’s hands were smooth and white.

“Roxy is right. Oliver it is,” good-natured Beely was saying. “He told me so himself, and he ought to know. Oliver Pope is the name of the fine big parcel I have brought.”

“But I thought there would be a letter,” repeated Roxy, still feeling very much surprised. “Instead, it is a boy.”

“There is a letter too,” was Oliver’s answer. “It is in

my pocket. It tells all about everything. It is for your mother."

Oliver hopped out of the mail car after Beely opened the door. By that time, Mrs. Hatfield had almost reached the gate.

Roxy, her cheeks red with excitement, ran for her father, at work in the shop.

"Come quick, Father," called Roxy. "Oliver is here, and Mother is reading her letter. 'See letter,' you know—Beely is waiting to hear the news too."

The letter from Oliver's father explained everything. But Oliver couldn't wait. He told most of the news before the letter could be read.

"I had to come so soon," said Oliver, "because my father is sailing for England tonight. And Margaret, my nurse, went away in a hurry yesterday because her daughter is sick. My father said I mustn't be a bother to you. He said he was sorry that he had to send me this way so soon."

"We are not sorry," answered Mrs. Hatfield quickly. "We are glad that you are here."

"We like company in this house," said Roxy's father, taking Oliver's bag from the car. "We never call them a 'bother,' especially if they are little boys."

"Well, Roxy, didn't I bring you a fine parcel?" asked Beely, starting his car. "But I didn't see any stamps on it, did you?"

"Stamps on a boy," said Oliver, laughing at the

thought.

Everyone was so pleasant and friendly. Already he began to feel at home.

"Come with me, Oliver," said Roxy, leading the way into the house. "You didn't come a minute too soon. Your room is all ready. I helped. After dinner, I will show you the barn and the brook and everything. You may have one of Claribel's eggs for supper if you like."

Roxy was as good as her word.

That afternoon, she and Oliver played in the brook. They visited the chickens. She showed Oliver every nook and cranny of the old red barn.

“This is a big barn,” said Oliver, looking about. “You have one, two, three stalls. Who lives in them?”

“Poky, our cow, has this stall,” answered Roxy, pointing. “There is no one in the other two. They are empty.”

“There is plenty of room, then, for a pony,” said Oliver. “At home, I ride in the park. My father said in his letter that I might have a pony here, if I liked.”

“A pony, Oliver! A pony!” Roxy turned with a whirl. “I saw a pony yesterday that could dance and walk backwards and run on three legs. His name is Calico. Why don’t you tell Father that Calico is the pony you want?”

“Is he a saddle pony?” asked Oliver, his eyes very bright. “I never rode a pony that could dance and do tricks.”

“He is the prettiest pony you ever saw,” said Roxy earnestly, “all black and white. I know you can ride him. I would rather have him than any other pony in all the world.”

“So would I,” agreed Oliver, as excited now as Roxy. “I’d like a black and white pony. I like the name Calico too. I do want Calico for my pony. Are you sure he can do tricks and dance?”

CHAPTER 4
WE WANT CALICO

Up the mountain went Mrs. Jingle, rattling merrily along the road. She was carrying Oliver and Roxy and Mr. Hatfield toward Rocky Farm.

For Oliver had been right about his father's letter. Mr. Pope had written that Oliver might have a pony while he stayed in the country. He had said that Roxy should ride the pony too.

"We can hire one for the summer from Farmer Drake," said Mr. Hatfield.

"I hope it will be Calico," answered Oliver. "I want Calico, and Roxy does too."

Now they had almost reached the farm. They were riding past Farmer Drake's meadow, where his ponies were galloping with flying tails or busily nibbling the green grass.

The car whirled through the wide gate of the pony yard.

Farmer Drake stood waiting for them. Three ponies were with him. One of them was dusty brown, one was sorrel color, and the third was black and white. All three ponies stared at the visitors with bright alert eyes.

"So the little boy wants a pony," was Farmer Drake's greeting to Mr. Hatfield. "I told you over the telephone that I had three good ponies to choose from, and here they are. This one is Lassie. This lively fellow is named Mustard. And here is Calico, who went calling on Roxy the other day."

At the sound of his name, Calico pricked up his ears. He stamped on the ground with a neat little hoof.

"Thump! Thump! Thump!" went Calico.

Then he tossed his head and arched his glossy neck.

"He calls for his breakfast with those thumps," said Farmer Drake, laughing. "Calico is a first-rate, all-round saddle pony. He can pull a little cart, too."

"We want Calico," began Oliver. "Roxy, you speak up and tell what you saw."

"We want Calico because he can do tricks," said Roxy eagerly. "I saw him, and I know."

"I have never seen any tricks," said the farmer. "But you couldn't do better than to take Calico. My grandson, Billy, likes him best of all the ponies. He calls him 'his pony,' he likes Calico so well."

"Suppose Oliver takes a ride on each pony," suggested Mr. Hatfield. "Then he will know which one he really wants."

So Oliver mounted Lassie, and round and round the

pony yard and round about the farmhouse they went.

Lassie was a mouse-like pony. Her coat was mouse-colored too. She looked as gentle as a great Newfoundland dog. She walked with a sober step. When Oliver shook the reins, she trotted nicely. Then she fell into a mild little walk again.

"She is a good pony," said Oliver, when the ride was over. "She would do for a scared little girl, I think. But she isn't a pony that a boy would like at all."

All this while, Mustard had been pulling at his bridle. He fidgeted and pawed the ground. It was plain that Mustard didn't like to wait.

With Oliver on his back, the sorrel pony set off at a good smart pace. He broke into a canter, and Oliver had to hold the reins tight. As Mustard wheeled around the house, Oliver's cap flew off. By the time they came dashing back, the little boy's cheeks were red, and he was quite out of breath.

"Lassie is too slow, and Mustard is too fast," gasped Oliver when he could speak.

"Try Calico, and see how he goes," was Farmer Drake's answer.

Off trotted Calico, steady yet fun.

At the end of the ride, Oliver made him whirl and turn about and then stand still.

"See! He does just what I tell him to do," said Oliver happily. "He is the best pony of all."

By this time, Roxy was dancing with impatience.

"Let me have a ride. It is my turn now," she cried.

So Roxy was lifted onto Calico's back. She patted his neck as he moved quietly off.

"Go on, Calico," called Roxy. "I won't be afraid if you run."

Calico seemed to understand. At least, he took Roxy at her word. He galloped, he trotted, he cantered. It was all great fun. Roxy was only sorry when Calico brought her back to the pony yard, and she had to slip to the ground.

Now was the time to choose the pony.

"We want Calico," said Oliver.

"Yes, we do," added Roxy.

So it was settled.

"A little green cart goes with your pony," Farmer Drake told them. "He knows how to pull a cart."

"A cart? I can drive a cart," said Oliver quickly. "I learned in the park."

“Then you would like to drive Calico home now,” said the farmer. “Just wait until I take these other two ponies back to the pasture. I want to ride with you this first time to see that everything is safe.”

Away drove Mr. Hatfield with Mrs. Jingle.

Off trotted Lassie and Mustard with Farmer Drake. They did not care that they had not been chosen. You could tell by the happy pounding of their little hoofs.

This left Calico and Roxy and Oliver alone in the pony yard.

It was then that Calico showed what he could do if he liked. It was quite unexpected. Oliver and Roxy were taken by surprise.

For suddenly, Calico rose on his hind legs. Round and round and round he turned in a dance.

Down he came to the ground again. There was a merry look in his brown eyes. He stamped playfully and flourished his tail as the children stared.

“There, Oliver! I told you so,” exclaimed Roxy, delighted. “Now you have seen one of his tricks too. Isn’t it true that he dances? Wasn’t that a dance?”

“Of course it was a dance,” answered Oliver joyfully. “I hope he will show us his other tricks too.”

Oliver looked happy as he patted Calico and rubbed his long nose. What a pony! What fun he was going to be!

“Here comes Farmer Drake,” said Roxy. “Let’s run and tell him what happened.”

But at the great news, Farmer Drake only shook his head.

“Dance, did he?” said the farmer, smiling at the children. “Well, you call me the next time he begins his dancing. I want to see it with my own eyes.”

Then Farmer Drake brought out a brush and currycomb.

“These will make your pony’s coat smooth and shiny,” he said to Oliver. “You must learn how to use them.”

“Me? Can I take care of my pony?” cried Oliver. “I thought I would have to have a groom.”

At this, Roxy put back her head and laughed. The farmer smiled too.

“A groom!” said Roxy, still laughing. “Father is the only groom at our house.”

“Mr. Hatfield will tell you what to feed Calico and how to keep his stall clean,” said Farmer Drake. “But you can take care of your own pony.”

“I want to do everything for Calico,” said Oliver proudly. “Perhaps I will let Roxy help a little. But I will be the only boy I know who takes care of a pony all by himself.”

Now came the harnessing of Calico to the cart. It was a shining green cart with bright yellow wheels.

Calico seemed used to his harness. He didn’t mind

the bit in his mouth at all. He let Farmer Drake fasten straps and buckles as if he knew all about it. He backed between the shafts of the cart and stood quietly while the braces were made fast.

Into the cart climbed Roxy and Oliver. Oliver lifted the reins. They were off.

Farmer Drake, on his gray horse, Graceful, rode close behind.

Out of the pony yard stepped Calico, drawing the little cart. Round the corner they wheeled and into the road.

There Calico quickened his pace. Tip-tap, tip-tap, tip-tap went his four little hoofs. Merrily rolled the yellow wheels.

The road grew steep, and Calico slowed up. He held back the cart carefully. Down, down the mountain they went. Now they were nearly home.

"I wish," said Roxy, sitting very straight, "that everyone in Little Turkey could see us ride by."

In their own barnyard, with Mr. Hatfield looking on, Oliver and Roxy unharnessed Calico and led him into his stall.

"He is tired now. You must let him rest," said the farmer. "Goodbye, Calico. Goodbye and good luck."

To everyone's surprise, Calico answered.

"Whee-ee-ee!" he whinnied. "Whee-ee!"

They all laughed to hear him. It was as funny as it could be.

"We must tell Father how he danced for us this morning," said Roxy, when they were alone. "Farmer Drake doesn't believe he did it, I think. But you saw him, Oliver. You know it is true."

"Of course it is true," answered Oliver. "I am glad he is our pony for all summer. I do wonder who taught him how to dance."

CHAPTER 5

IN AND OUT THE RED BARN

Thump! Thump! Thump!

Thump! Thump! Bang!

It was Calico asking for his breakfast. Every morning, the children could hear him pounding in his stall.

Thump! Thump! Bang!

Calico was hungry. It was very hard to wait.

Out to the barn ran Oliver and Roxy.

"How he can pound!" said Oliver, proud of his pet.

Over Calico's willing head, he slipped a halter. Out of the stall, he led the pony straight to the watering trough in front of the barn.

"Take a good drink, Calico," said Oliver. "Then you shall have your breakfast."

Calico did as he was told. He buried his nose in the cool water. He took a long drink.

Now they were back in the barn. Into the pony's feed box went oats and three ears of corn and a little salt.

The hungry pony lost not a moment. He thrust his nose into the box. He munched busily. His tail swished with contentment.

Roxy was feeding the chickens. They pushed and squawked and crowded around her feet. Claribel pushed the hardest and squawked the loudest of them all.

"Father has fed and milked Poky," said Roxy, scattering her last handful of corn. "We will take her to pasture when Calico finishes his breakfast. It is your turn this morning to ride."

Morning and night Calico carried the children when they drove Poky to and from the pasture.

Now Calico was ready. The feed box was empty. Not even a grain of salt was left.

From the edge of the watering trough, Oliver jumped to the pony's back.

"Here we come," said Roxy, leading Poky out of the barn.

With a bark, Watch joined them, and they set off.

Down the country road they went, a boy and a pony, a girl and a cow, and a yellow collie dog.

The roadside was gay with bright buttercups and daisies and wild carrots nodding in the breeze.

They passed Beely's house. The blue front door was shut tight. The red chimney glistened in the sunshine. The green roof gleamed.

"See Mrs. Poole's garden," said Roxy with a wave

of the hand as they went along. "It is called an old-fashioned garden. Isn't it pretty? People come riding up here just to buy."

At the side of a small white house grew a beautiful garden. It was filled with old-fashioned flowers, as Roxy had said. There were fragrant mignonette and glowing snapdragon. The clove-scented stocks, pink and crimson and lavender, grew side by side with Sweet William and quiet heliotrope.

Mrs. Poole was weeding in the garden. She saw the children and waved to them as they passed.

"The next house is the Daggetts's," announced Roxy, nodding toward a gray cottage standing low under the trees. "There is Captain Daggett on the porch. He used to be a boat captain. Mrs. Daggett makes the best doughnuts you ever ate."

Across the road was Poky's pasture.

"Baw!" said Poky in a lonely voice when she was safely behind the great wooden gate. "Ba-a-aw!"

Roxy was hard-hearted and shook her head.

"Don't stand there looking at us over the fence," said she briskly. "You know you want to eat the nice grass. Goodbye! We are going down the road to see the Peters's pig."

"The Peters are poor," Roxy told Oliver as they turned their backs on Poky. "Their new pig is the very nicest thing they own."

There were four Peters children, and they all came out to see Calico and to show off Anna Maria, the new pig.

There were Lucy and Hannah and Jeff and Milly Minerva. Lucy was a fair, smiling little girl. Hannah was dark with a sober face. The little boy, Jeff, hopped about as lively as a cricket, while Milly Minerva, the baby, had all she could do to keep upon her feet. Milly Minerva was not quite two years old. Lucy was eight, and the other fitted in between.

Anna Maria, the pig, was pink and white with a double chin. She grunted and waved her nose with pleasure when the children scratched her back with a stick. Then she lay down in a corner of her pen and went to sleep. At least she didn't stir no matter how hard she was poked.

Now it was Calico's turn, and he behaved well, so Oliver thought. He pranced up the road, shaking his mane. He whirled around at the pull of the rein. Off he galloped with such a ringing of hoofs that Aunt Eliza Webb, who lived in the next house, peered out of her window in a fright.

"Well, I declare," said Aunt Eliza, shaking her head. "It is only Roxy's Oliver and that frisky calico pony. I thought 'twas an airplane landing right in my front yard."

Oliver came careering back at such a pace that all the Peters, even Milly Minerva, shouted at the sight. They made so much noise that Anna Maria opened one sleepy eye to see what was going on.

"Someday we will give you all a ride," promised Roxy. "Now we have to go home and work. We are both as busy as we can be."

What Roxy said was very true. She and Oliver had tasks that must not be left undone. It was not long before Roxy was up in the barn loft hunting for eggs. Oliver stood below, putting fresh straw in Calico's stall.

"I will tell you what I think," said Oliver as Roxy climbed down the stairs. "I am doing farmer's work, and I think I ought to wear farmer's clothes."

As he spoke, Oliver thrust his small pitchfork into the hay with a business-like air.

"You need overalls," answered Roxy promptly, "blue

overalls. That is what Father wears."

She set down her basket with care. It held five new eggs.

"Then overalls are what I want," said Oliver firmly, "and a farmer's hat too. And I am going barefoot. You do sometimes, and so will I. When can I buy my farmer clothes, Roxy? When are we going to town?"

Oliver was fast turning into a sturdy country boy. He was as brown as a nut, with as many scratches on his fingers and freckles on his nose as Roxy. He liked country work and country play. Best of all, he liked taking care of Calico. He fed and groomed his pony faithfully. Every day he cleaned his stall and made it neat with fresh straw.

Oliver was proud of his trust.

"I would never forget to feed Calico and take good care of him," he often thought. "It is lots more fun to have your own pony than to ride in the park with a groom."

Roxy was ready now to answer Oliver's question.

"Somebody ought to go to town this very afternoon," she said with a thoughtful air. "Mother has four dozen eggs to sell, I know. Some of the egg money, Oliver, is mine. I am saving to buy a bracelet. I get two cents for every one of Claribel's eggs."

"Ask your mother about going to town," called Oliver as Roxy carried her basket into the house.

In a very few moments, back came Roxy. A bright,

flowered work-bag swung from her arm.

Calico now stood in the middle of the barn floor. Oliver was hard at work on the pony's coat with brush and currycomb.

Roxy stopped in passing to give Calico a pat. She reached up to smooth his white star.

"Whoo! Whoo!" sneezed Calico suddenly.

It was a dusty little sneeze. It made the children laugh.

Roxy climbed up and seated herself on the edge of Calico's stall.

"Are we going to town?" asked Oliver, standing off to look at his work.

"I couldn't find Mother," answered Roxy, "but I borrowed her gold thimble for my sewing. She won't mind. It is the prettiest thimble. It has little gold flowers all around the edge."

Roxy opened her work-bag and took out her sewing. It was a bright and cheerful bit of work, striped red and white and green.

"This is going to be a Christmas present," announced Roxy. "It will be a shoe bag for Father, I think."

Roxy sewed and Oliver brushed without speaking. The barn was very quiet. Calico didn't even stamp his foot. The hens in the yard clucked peacefully as they pecked here and there.

Suddenly the barnyard was in an uproar.

Over the stone wall came Watch, barking loudly. He was chasing something. It was something small and yellow and striped.

The noise startled everyone.

The hens scattered. They ran wildly with fluttering wings. They squawked shrilly. Claribel fairly shrieked.

Calico was frightened. He backed and turned and darted into his stall. This left Oliver staring, with the currycomb fallen from his hand.

As for Roxy, she came tumbling down from the edge of the stall with a bump. Her work-bag flew one way, her scissors another. Mr. Hatfield's Christmas present went flying into a milk pail. Fortunately, the pail was clean and dry.

In the meantime, the something small and yellow and striped had vanished under the wall. Watch could only dance back and forth and paw at the stones and bark.

Roxy was the first to speak.

"It is all Watch's fault," said she crossly, picking herself up. "He was chasing a poor little chipmunk. I saw him. Where is my sewing? I must go back to work."

But a moment later, Roxy began to call out and run wildly back and forth.

"It's gone! It's gone!" cried Roxy. "I can't find it anywhere. It is lost. Help me, Oliver! Help me! My mother's gold thimble is lost."

CHAPTER 6

LOST—A GOLD THIMBLE

"There is no use looking any longer, Oliver," said Roxy in a doleful voice. "My mother's gold thimble is lost for good."

Slowly Oliver rose from the floor of Calico's stall. He had done his best to help Roxy find the thimble. The clean straw had been pulled from the pony's stall and lay scattered about.

"We have looked everywhere," admitted Oliver. "I know the thimble isn't in Calico's stall. I was sure it bounced in there, Roxy, when you fell down."

Outside the barn door, Calico gave a soft whinny. Perhaps he wanted to comfort his two friends, who at that moment looked very sad.

"It is gone, I tell you," said Roxy mournfully. "Oh, dear! Oh, dear! I wish I hadn't touched the thimble. I must go tell Mother what has happened. I wish I could run away."

By this time, Roxy's eyes were full of tears. When she left the barn, she was crying out loud. Mrs.

Hatfield must have known something was wrong long before Roxy reached the house.

But, soon, back to the barn came Roxy, and with her were both Mr. and Mrs. Hatfield.

"The thimble was a birthday present from your father," said Mrs. Hatfield, searching busily. "We must find it. It must be here."

A birthday present! Roxy already felt sorry. But when she heard this, she felt much worse.

Now the red barn was given a searching such as it had never known before. But in spite of this, the thimble was not found. At last even Mrs. Hatfield gave up looking. The thimble seemed gone, as Roxy said, "for good."

But as she searched, Roxy had been thinking. Now she stepped forward. She had something to say. She was winking fast, but she did not shed a single tear.

"I know what to do," said Roxy. "I will take my egg money and buy Mother a new thimble. I was saving up for a bracelet. I have thirty-two cents. But I will buy Mother a gold thimble in town instead. I will save and save until I have enough."

Everyone looked at Roxy. At last her father spoke. He sounded so kind that at once Roxy felt better. She knew that he understood.

"That seems fair to me," said Mr. Hatfield slowly. "You lost the thimble and, of course, you want to pay."

"Yes, I do," answered Roxy.

And she meant what she said.

So that afternoon, as the very first step toward buying the thimble, the children were to drive Calico into town.

"Calico is steady, and Oliver is a careful driver," said Mr. Hatfield, thinking it over. "You will do your errands and come straight home again."

After dinner, off they started.

Down the road rolled the bright cart. At Roxy's feet stood a big basket. It was carefully packed with boxes of eggs. Calico trotted merrily as if he were enjoying the trip.

Far off rose a wide ring of misty blue mountains. Close at hand, Old Moody looked cool and green, shadowy and dark. The sky was dotted with great white billowing clouds.

On and on they sped along the brown country road. The “thank-you-marms” didn’t bother Calico. He knew when to pull and when to hold back. Now and then, a noisy automobile went roaring by. Not that Calico seemed to mind. Soberly, he drew aside into the ditch.

But when the road was level and clear, how steadily and swiftly the little calico pony trotted along! Roxy was surprised to catch sight of the roofs and spires and chimneys of town so soon.

"Look, Oliver!" she exclaimed. "See those three church steeples? That is town."

So it was, and a neat, pleasant little town it proved to be.

It seemed a busy place to country Roxy. Even Oliver, who knew the bustling crowds of New York, stared at the people and the stores and the automobiles. As for Calico, his little hoofs rang out a brisk tune on the hard paving. He answered every pull of the reins. But what he thought of it all, no one could say.

Round about town drove the children. First, they left the eggs at the grocery. Next, in the jewelry shop, they priced a whole tray of gold thimbles. Last of all, they drove to the Emporium, a big general store, where overalls, as well as almost everything else, were sold.

So well and so quickly did they do their errands that it was not long before Calico was trotting back over the road toward home.

"We sold the eggs just as Mother told us, didn't we?" chattered Roxy, comfortably swinging her feet in the empty egg basket. "The grocery man knew Mother well, he said. Isn't it wonderful that the jeweler has a thimble almost exactly like Mother's? It will cost four dollars. But how bright it shines!"

Oliver nodded happily. He felt very proud. He looked unusually plump as well. This was because he had pulled on his new overalls over his suit. He couldn't wait until he reached home. His new straw hat, too, flapped against his ears. Oliver liked the wide hat with the blue ribbon. Better still, he liked the long trousers that reached to his ankles.

"I look like a man now," he was thinking. "I look like Farmer Drake."

When Calico came trotting back into Little Turkey, Aunt Eliza Webb, plump and rosy, was standing at her front gate. She must have been watching for the children, for she waved as soon as they drove in sight.

"Wait a minute, children," called Aunt Eliza. "I have something for Roxy to take home."

Indoors stepped Aunt Eliza.

Back she came. In her arms she carried a kitten, a yellow tortoise-shell kitten.

"Here is the little ginger cat I promised you, Roxy," said Aunt Eliza with a smile. "My niece brought him from over the mountain this afternoon. He is a right good little cat, she says. He won't run away if you are careful to butter his feet."

Into Roxy's lap went the ginger kitten. He was a round little cat with a round head and a mouth that seemed to smile.

Straight up the front of Roxy's dress he climbed. When he reached her shoulder, he perched there. Roxy heard a loud humming. The ginger kitten had begun to purr.

"He likes me," said Roxy, delighted. "He is happy.

See his little cat smile. What is his name, Aunt Eliza? Did your niece tell?"

"She called him 'kitty,'" answered Aunt Eliza. "You must give him a name."

"I would like to name him 'Eliza' for you," said Roxy. "But I don't suppose he would want a girl's name. What was Mr. Webb's name?"

"Silas," answered Aunt Eliza, laughing, "Silas Ebenezer Webb."

"I like the name Silas," said Roxy, looking pleased. "That is what I am going to call my cat."

And as Calico moved off, Roxy called back to Aunt Eliza, "I won't forget about Silas's paws. I will butter them myself tonight."

If Calico felt tired at the end of this long and busy afternoon, he didn't show it. Instead, he behaved in such a lively fashion that you might have thought he had just woken up from a long night's sleep.

They were in the barnyard, Oliver and Roxy, Silas and Calico. Calico had been unharnessed. He had taken a long cool drink and a refreshing mouthful of grass.

Silas sat on Roxy's shoulder. As they stood there, she reached up and placed the kitten on Calico's back. There he perched, a yellow dot against the glossy black and white of the pony's coat.

It was then that Calico moved off, carrying the kitten. Faster and faster he went until he was galloping around the yard.

"Look, Oliver, look! It is the trick!" cried Roxy. "It is one of the tricks I told you about."

So it was! Calico was galloping swiftly on three legs, instead of four.

But this was not all.

Up went Calico on his hind feet. Silas held fast. Back, back, back stepped Calico.

The children stared. They neither spoke nor moved.

Then round and round went Calico with small dancing steps, round and round and round.

The pony tossed his head as if he were enjoying himself.

Silas clung like a burr. His eyes looked wild, but he held on tight. This was something that had never happened before to the ginger kitten.

It was all over in a very few moments. Calico was back on the ground again, looking as if nothing had happened. With a leap, Silas landed on all four feet. Off he scampered into the barn where he fell to playing with a long wisp of hay.

"Now you have seen all the tricks too," cried Roxy, dancing with excitement. "You have seen all three of Calico's tricks."

"Where did he learn them?" asked Oliver, his eyes round with wonder. "Other ponies don't do such things. Calico, you tell us. You tell us who taught you your tricks."

But Calico only pawed the ground and whinnied and looked about him with a mischievous air.

Oliver sat down to think it over. But at the end of all his thinking, he knew no more than he did before.

As for Roxy, exciting as this was, her mind was soon filled with other thoughts.

“I must remember to butter Silas’s toes tonight,” Roxy was thinking. “And I must ask Father how long it will take to earn the gold thimble at two cents an egg.”

CHAPTER 7

THE DRIVE WITHOUT END

Autumn had come, and wherever you looked, the world was aflame. The sugar maple trees blazed scarlet and gold against a deep blue sky. Old Moody had put on a many-colored coat of russet and orange and crimson, with dark patches here and there where the evergreens grew.

Roxy sat on the porch steps. She was talking to Silas, who was sunning himself at her feet.

"We are all alone in the house, Silas," said Roxy. "Mother and Father have gone over the mountain. You and I have to spend the afternoon with Aunt Eliza. Mother told me I must."

Silas yawned and showed his pink tongue. That was his only answer. But Roxy had other news to tell.

"Oliver will be home tonight," went on Roxy. "He has been away on a visit. Did you know, Silas, that Oliver was going to stay here with us this winter? Perhaps he will be here all next summer, too."

This was quite true. Mr. Pope had written that

business might keep him in England throughout the winter. And it had been settled that Oliver was to stay in Little Turkey until his father came home.

Silas rose and stretched himself. But before he could take a step, Roxy picked him up in her arms.

"Here come the Peters children," said Roxy. "Let's go down to the gate and talk."

On the way to the gate, an idea came to Roxy. It was a pleasant idea, she thought.

"Wouldn't you like to go driving?" called Roxy to the children. "I will take you for a drive with Calico and the cart."

Of course, the Peterses wanted to go driving. They knew where they wanted to go too.

"Take us to see Grandma Peters," they pleaded. "Grandma makes ginger cakes. She keeps a jarful. Oh, Roxy, drive us to see Grandma, do!"

Roxy nodded gaily. She wanted everyone to have a good time. She had forgotten that she was to go to Aunt Eliza's. It had gone completely out of her head.

"Yes, I will," agreed Roxy. "Where does your Grandma live? Is it far? Do you know the way?"

"It is on the old back road, and you go over two bridges," answered Lucy.

"The road is steep, and there are lots of stones," said Hannah.

"The house is white. It isn't very far," added Jeff, hopping with joy at the thought of the ride.

"Grandma! Cakes!" said Milly Minerva happily as she followed the children out to the barn.

It is true that on the way Milly Minerva sat down suddenly more than once. But she didn't seem to mind. She only picked herself up again and hurried on.

"I can harness Calico," said Roxy briskly. "I know how. You help me pull out the cart."

In no time, Calico was harnessed to the green cart. In climbed the children. Silas went too. He was wedged between Roxy and Milly Minerva. It was a very tight squeeze.

Roxy took up the reins, and off they started. Calico trotted out of the barnyard and straight down the road. His ears winked merrily. His hoofs pounded out a tune.

"It is easy to drive," said Roxy airily. "But, of course, you have to know how."

The truth was Roxy herself didn't know very much about driving. She had driven Calico only three or four times and then not very far. It was Oliver who held the reins. And Calico knew the difference. Oliver was a steady driver. Roxy tugged and jerked.

But on went Calico. He turned into the back road at Roxy's bidding.

It was a lonely road. There were few houses to be seen. On either side lay fields, steep and stony. Round about rose the Vermont hills, bright with the red and yellow sugar maple trees.

On they rode, uphill and down, for a long, long time, or so it seemed to Roxy. Her arms ached from pulling at the reins.

Every now and then, Lucy would say hopefully, "I think Grandma's house is just the other side of this next hill."

But no, it was never there. Never did they see anything that looked like Grandma Peters's house.

After a while, Hannah and Lucy looked troubled. Where was Grandma's house? Had they taken the wrong road?

"Let's turn around and go home," suggested Hannah.

But Roxy shook her head.

She felt discouraged.

"I can't," said Roxy. "I am afraid we will tip over. I don't know how to turn around."

Unless they met someone who would help them, they must drive on until they found the house.

Suddenly, on a hilltop, Calico stood still. He wouldn't move, no matter what Roxy did or said. You see, the pulling on the reins hurt his mouth. The heavy cart tired him. Calico needed a rest.

It was at this moment that Silas gave a sudden spring and leaped from the pony cart. Into the bushes he bounded and out of sight.

Roxy stared after him in dismay.

This was too dreadful. Suppose Silas never found his way home again!

"Oh, Calico," called Roxy in a piteous voice, "Silas is gone, and I can't run after him. Won't you go on and take us to Grandma Peters? You know I can't turn round."

Roxy flapped the reins with all her might. And Calico, rested now, gave a heave and a pull and was off again.

But where was Grandma Peters's white house? Where was the jar of ginger cakes?

The road grew more wild and lonely. There was not

a house in sight.

By this time everyone was tired and disappointed. The little children grew fretful.

"I don't like to go riding," said Jeff. "I want to go home."

His face puckered. He looked ready to cry.

"Home! Home!" echoed Milly Minerva, putting out her under lip.

"We can't go home," returned Lucy sharply. "We have to find Grandma Peters's first."

"Perhaps we will never go home," added Hannah in a gloomy voice. "Roxy can't turn round."

At this bad news, Jeff and Milly Minerva began to cry in earnest. They wailed dismally as the cart bumped down a stony hill.

Now a fresh trouble befell them. Calico went lame. He limped painfully. There was something wrong with his right front foot.

Calico walked so slowly it almost seemed as if they didn't move.

Where were they? Where were they going?

No one knew.

Roxy let Calico follow the winding, twisting road. There was nothing else to do.

But now the road was leading them downhill.

Suddenly Lucy called out and pointed.

"Look!" cried Lucy. "Isn't that the quarry?"

Sure enough, beside the road was an old marble

quarry. It had not been used in many a year. The children knew the quarry well. It was not a mile from Little Turkey.

How had they come there?

It was not hard to guess.

The road had led them round in a great circle, and now it was taking them back home.

"Oh, Calico, we are going home. We are nearly there," called Roxy.

At the sound of his name, brave little Calico pricked up his ears. But he couldn't hurry. He could only limp slowly along. This ride would never come to an end, Roxy thought.

But at last her house was in sight.

At the gate stood Oliver, back from his visit. There stood Mr. and Mrs. Hatfield. All three faces wore an anxious, troubled look.

Oliver came running to meet them. He was angry, it was plain to see.

"What have you done to my pony?" he demanded. "He is lame. What have you done, Roxy? Where have you been?"

Roxy wouldn't answer. She shut her lips tight. Oliver needn't speak so, she thought, when she had had such a dreadful afternoon.

At last the gate was reached. Everyone was looking at Roxy. No one spoke. They were waiting to hear what had happened.

So Roxy began her story. It was not an easy story to tell.

When she had finished, Mr. Hatfield lifted her to the ground.

“Go indoors with your mother,” he said.

That was all he said. But Roxy knew what everyone was thinking. She didn’t have to be told.

“Everyone is scolding me,” thought Roxy, “even if they don’t speak a word.”

Even Calico turned his head away, or so it seemed.

Roxy was glad to eat her supper alone on the end of the kitchen table. She was glad to go straight to bed.

There she lay. She felt very unhappy. She was thinking over all that had happened. What a miserable, miserable time it had been!

The door opened, and in came her mother.

“Mother! Mother!” cried Roxy, sitting up and holding out her arms. “It was a horrid drive. I have hurt Calico, and nobody loves me, and I didn’t mind you, and Oliver is angry.”

Then Roxy’s mother talked to her. What she said was so true that Roxy agreed with every word she spoke.

“You must learn to be more thoughtful,” ended Mrs. Hatfield. “Father says that you must not ride Calico for one whole week.”

Roxy nodded sadly. She felt that this was only just and right.

Then Roxy was left to go to sleep.

But slowly, slowly the door was swinging open. Gently, gently four little feet came padding across the floor. With a spring and a thud, something landed on the bed.

It was Silas. He was smiling his little cat smile.

Softly he patted Roxy's cheek with his paw. Then he curled himself into a ball. He began to purr. It was a song of triumph. Silas had found his way home.

"Oh, Silas, Silas, I thought I should never see you again," cried Roxy, cuddling her kitten close. "But you did come home. It is because I buttered your paws. Calico only had a stone in his shoe, Silas. And Mother says Oliver isn't angry with me anymore."

Then Roxy lifted Silas and whispered in his ear.

"I am never, never going to drive Calico again without asking," said Roxy. "You wait and see."

CHAPTER 8

THE TRAVELING CHRISTMAS TREE

The ground was covered with snow. The tips of the tree branches were white. Old Moody wore a pointed nightcap. All this was as it should be, for it was Christmas Eve. And everyone knows that a white Christmas is the very best Christmas of all.

For many weeks Roxy and Oliver had been busy making ready for the happiest, jolliest holiday in the whole year. All Little Turkey was to come and spend Christmas Day at the Hatfields'. Everyone, that is, who was not going away.

Beely was coming for Christmas dinner. Captain and Mrs. Daggett were coming. So were Mr. and Mrs. Peters and the four children, Lucy and Hannah, Jeff and Milly Minerva.

There was to be a Christmas tree. Mr. Hatfield had cut it down, and Oliver and Roxy had helped drag it home.

It was not a very large tree, but it couldn't help being bright and beautiful, for the children had strung long chains of scarlet cranberries and snowy popcorn to twine among its branches. They had gilded and silvered walnuts and pine cones without number to use as ornaments.

Mrs. Hatfield had baked gingerbread boys and girls and funny gingerbread animals to hang upon the fragrant green boughs. There were cornucopias filled with homemade candy.

This was a homemade Christmas tree, and the children liked it all the better for that.

The Christmas presents were ready, too.

There was a rag doll for Milly Minerva. Mr. Hatfield had made out of wood a workbox for Lucy, a doll's trunk for Hannah, and a funny jumping jack for Jeff. These presents the children had painted in the brightest colors they could find.

"They are all beautiful," said Roxy happily.

And Oliver, well satisfied with these homemade Christmas presents, agreed.

Now, on Christmas Eve, all was ready. The little tree, glittering and glowing like a Christmas star, stood in its place.

"We have nothing to do but look at the tree and think about Christmas," said Roxy when the supper dishes were out of the way.

But at that very moment, Beely was walking up the front path. He brought news that gave everyone something to think about besides Christmas and the cheerful little tree.

"All the Peters have the mumps," announced Beely the moment he set foot in the house. "Mr. Peters called it out to me when I came riding by tonight. He told me to tell you as soon as I could."

"Can't they come tomorrow?" asked Oliver in dismay. "Won't they see the tree?"

"The presents!" exclaimed Roxy. "The doll in the pink dress! The jumping jack! The workbox! The little trunk! Can't we give the presents tomorrow at all?"

"Not one of them can set foot outdoors," was Beely's reply. "It is doctor's orders. Everybody has to stay in the house."

The poor Peters family! Mumps at Christmas! And the Christmas party! It wouldn't be half so much fun with the Peters away. Everyone looked sober. What a disappointment, on Christmas Eve too!

But it was not long before Roxy and Oliver sat whispering in a corner. Plainly there was something brewing. A new Christmas secret was in the air.

"We are thinking out a plan," Roxy couldn't help telling her father when she said goodnight. "You will know it tomorrow."

Christmas Day was all that the children had hoped it would be. It was clear and bright with a snap in the air.

Before daybreak, Roxy and Oliver crept downstairs to find their presents under the Christmas tree.

"A bracelet, a silver bracelet!" cried happy Roxy, slipping it on her wrist at once.

"Skis!" exclaimed Oliver, hugging a long, awkward armful. "I will come down Old Moody in these skis in two jumps, maybe one."

Now in the cold starlight, the children ran out to the barn.

"I wonder whether Poky kneeled down last night," said Roxy.

She was thinking of the Christmas legend that told how the cattle kneel at midnight on Christmas Eve.

Oliver was carrying a basket.

"I hope Calico likes his Christmas present," he said.

Stamp! Bang! went Calico's hoof when the barn door was opened.

"He is saying 'Merry Christmas!'" called Roxy. "Merry Christmas, Calico! Merry Christmas, Poky!"

Poky was awake. She stared at Roxy with great kind eyes.

There was no telling whether she had kneeled at midnight or no. But she seemed glad of the armful of sweet hay that Roxy gave her.

"Here is a Christmas present, Calico," said Oliver, standing in front of the pony. "It is what we thought you would like best of all."

Into Calico's willing mouth, one by one, went three bright red apples, four golden carrots, and six lumps of sugar.

Roxy held the basket. Oliver fed him. And by the way Calico munched his goodies, the children felt sure that he was pleased with his Christmas treat.

It was at the Christmas breakfast table that the children told their secret.

"You tell, Oliver," urged Roxy. "You thought of it first."

So Oliver told.

"We want to take the Christmas tree traveling down to the Peters," said Oliver. "We want to take the Peters their presents too."

"We will leave them outside the door," interrupted Roxy. "We won't go in."

"We must take the tree too," repeated Oliver. "It won't seem like Christmas Day to the Peters if they don't see the tree."

"We have thought out just how to do it," broke in Roxy again. "We can put the tree on the big sled, and Calico can pull it. It will be a traveling Christmas tree. That is what we call it. A traveling Christmas tree!"

Strange as it might seem, this is just what happened. The little tree went traveling. And this is how it went.

First of all, up to the gate stepped Calico, drawing the broad low sled.

Such a Christmas pony you never, never saw!

To begin with, he was brushed until he shone like satin. Oliver had seen to that. His foretop was tied with a bright red ribbon. That was Roxy's doing. But, more than that, over each ear was stuck a spray of holly. It gave Calico the gayest kind of a holiday look.

Calico's head was high. His brown eyes were bright and happy. They held a look of mischief too.

Then out came the little Christmas tree. Carefully Mr. Hatfield placed it on the sled. He braced it and made it firm with logs of wood.

Round about the tree were placed the Peters's Christmas presents. There was a great basket of Christmas dinner too.

The little tree glittered bravely in the morning sunshine. It stood straight and firm as Calico stepped slowly down the road. The snow squeaked under the sled runners. The twigs overhead snapped with the cold.

On went Calico. Oliver walked at his head. Roxy guarded the tree. The sled moved smoothly along the ruts in the frozen road.

Here was the Peters's cottage. Milly Minerva, from her bed by the window, was the first to see them coming. In a twinkling she was on her feet, her nose pressed flat against the glass.

Now, here were the other children beside her, Lucy and Hannah and Jeff.

Such a funny sight they were, all four of them! Their cheeks were swollen as round as balloons. Jeff's nose was pushed sideways. Poor Hannah couldn't open one eye.

But in spite of all this, when Roxy and Oliver called "Merry Christmas!" the Peters children answered in hoarse but happy croaks.

Mr. and Mrs. Peters were hastily tucking shawls and blankets around the excited children.

Who wouldn't be excited to see a Christmas tree, all gold and silver and scarlet and snowy-white, come riding down the road and stop at the gate?

Now, from under the tree, came a dolly dressed in pink. Milly Minerva laughed aloud as best she could and held out her arms at the sight.

Out came a lively jumping jack. Oliver made him leap and dance to the great joy of little Jeff, who, forgetting where he was, tried to jump and dance too.

The next present was a green workbox with a red

Christmas rose painted on it.

"For me? I love to sew," croaked Lucy, trying to smile in spite of her too-plump cheeks.

Here was the doll's trunk, a rich yellow, tastefully trimmed with brown stripes and dots. Hannah was so delighted that she forgot her troubles and beat upon the window louder than anyone else.

Now for the great basket of Christmas dinner. It took both Oliver and Roxy to lift it from the sled.

Down from the tree came the gingerbread goodies, the horns filled with candy.

"It isn't pucker candy, like lemon drops," called Roxy, who had had the mumps. "You needn't be afraid to eat it, not one bit."

There the presents stood, spread out in front of the window, on the dry crisp snow.

What a Christmas! The pale little Peters in the window clapped their hands for joy. They could not go for their Christmas, but Christmas had come to them.

Mr. and Mrs. Peters were nodding and laughing. The children waved and pounded on the pane.

The traveling Christmas tree was a great success!

Slowly Calico turned and moved off.

"There comes Mr. Peters out to get the presents," said Oliver, looking back.

Now, just around the corner, a surprise was waiting for Oliver and Roxy. After all, you could hardly blame Calico for wanting a little Christmas fun.

Round the turn in the road went Calico.

One moment, he was trudging past Beely's gate as sober and steady as a pony could be.

The next moment, he was flying up the road in the gayest, most carefree kind of a way. The little tree rocked and swayed as Calico sped past his own gateway and pounded on over the bridge.

"Stop! Stop!" cried Oliver.

He stood still in the road to stare at the runaway pony. Then he ran after Calico as fast as he could go.

Beely saw it all from his doorway. It wasn't long before Beely and Roxy were running up the road.

You could see the runaway plainly. The sled bumped along in and out of the snowy ruts. The little tree shook and swayed, but it did not fall.

On went Calico. He tossed his head gaily. His tail blew out in the wind. He fairly seemed to prance.

Would he ever stop? Where was he going?

On and on he ran.

At last, when everyone was out of breath, suddenly Calico stood still.

His front legs were buried in a snowdrift. His breath steamed on the frosty air. The sled was turned halfway across the road. But the little tree was still upright. It was shaken. Its boughs were quivering. A few popcorn chains had fallen. But no real harm had been done after all.

"Why, Calico!" exclaimed Oliver, when he reached

his pony. “Why, Calico, what made you act this way?”

Beely and Roxy, now, were there too.

Calico rolled a mischievous eye round at Oliver.

“Just for fun,” his look seemed to say.

Then he stared thoughtfully under a big oak tree nearby. The snow was covered with tiny footprints, more than you could count.

“Squirrels,” said Roxy and Oliver in a breath.

“He wants us to give the squirrels a Christmas present,” added Roxy quickly. “We can break the gingerbread cookies into bits.”

So, leaving a present on the snow for the squirrels, home they started.

On the way, Beely was told about the traveling Christmas tree.

“That is why Calico ran away,” said Beely. “He likes traveling, and the trip in Little Turkey wasn’t enough.”

“I think he did it so the squirrels would have some Christmas,” said Roxy.

But Oliver didn’t agree.

“He ran away for fun,” said Oliver, “and because he was happy. He was excited too. I think he knows that we are the first people in the world to have a traveling Christmas tree.”

CHAPTER 9
SUGARING TIME

“Roxy, what does the turn of the year mean?” Oliver stood still in the snow to ask this question. “Your father said this morning that sugaring always came at the turn of the year.”

It was Saturday morning, and Roxy and Oliver were slipping and sliding through ice and slush up a snowy hillside. They were on their way to the sugar-maple grove where Mr. Hatfield was busily at work.

“The turn of the year is when the seasons change. Don’t you know that?” answered Roxy, glad to tell. “Sugaring comes when the year turns away from winter and turns toward spring. It will be spring now before we know it. The sun feels so warm.”

“I know the warm sun makes plenty of slush,” replied Oliver, taking one step forward and slipping back two. “If we didn’t ride to school on Calico, we wouldn’t get there at all. Mrs. Jingle can’t take us. Didn’t she get stuck twice in the drifts? We would have to stay home.”

All Oliver said was true. At the turn of the year, now, the days were longer. At noon the silver icicles dripped. The snow on the roads was growing soft. Sturdy Calico carried both the children to school on his back. Now and then he slumped up to his knees in the wayside drifts. But he was as steady and safe as any old Dobbin. Never yet had the children fallen from his back.

At the turn of the year, too, the sap was rising in the trees. It was time to make maple syrup. Mr. Hatfield had been at work for days in his grove of sugar maples on the hill.

On went the children, nimbly jumping over the icy puddles. It was not long before they reached Mr. Hatfield and the clump of sugar-maple trees.

Here a big bonfire burned with a cheerful crackle. The children were glad to warm their stiff fingers at the blaze.

Over the fire hung a great iron kettle. Into the kettle Mr. Hatfield was emptying buckets of sap.

Roxy felt at home here in her father's woods.

"Come and see the trees, Oliver," she said, leading the way. "I can tell you all about it. I know just what Father does."

So Roxy showed Oliver where in every tree trunk a small hole had been bored and a little wooden spout fitted into it. Drip, drip, drip from each spout into a small hanging pail came the sweet maple sap.

"Then Father empties the little pails into a big one," explained Roxy. "See, he is doing it now. Perhaps we can help. Then he pours the big pailful into the kettle, and it boils and boils and boils."

All morning long Oliver and Roxy stayed in the maple wood. They helped in every way that they could. They threw wood on the fire to keep the great kettle boiling. They emptied the ice-cold sap from the small pails into the large one. They tasted the sweet sap, too, time and time again.

"It is thin, like water," said Oliver, taking a long, long sip. "I like the hot syrup better after it is boiled thick."

"This syrup isn't thick," said Roxy with a knowing air. "Wait until Mother boils it down at home."

That was what happened next. The hot syrup was carried down the hill and set to boil on the kitchen stove. The room was filled with the sweet odor and the sound of bubbling in the great boiling pot.

"I must go back to the maple grove," said Mr. Hatfield when dinner was over. "It takes forty gallons of sap to make one gallon of syrup. Remember that."

And swinging his empty kettle, he started up the hill.

Oliver and Roxy didn't go with him. They stayed at home to help Mrs. Hatfield, they said.

"When the syrup is thick enough, Mother will pour it into pans to cool," said Roxy, watching the great heaving, bubbling pots. "When the pans are empty, we will scrape them."

Now it may be that the children already had had too many 'tastes' of the sweet syrup. There must have been some reason why, a little later, they became so cross.

On the back porch stood the row of pans, cooling in the sharp winter air. Nearby, on one barnyard gatepost, sat Roxy. On the other post perched Oliver. They both had their eyes fixed on the cooling pans.

Watch and Silas had been shut in the barn to keep them out of mischief. Watch was howling dismally.

Silas had lost his little cat smile.

Calico was wandering about the barnyard. He whinnied softly. It was a pleasant, friendly sound. As Roxy and Oliver turned to look at him, Calico backed up against a post. He meant to have a tail-rub. He braced his four little legs and pushed back. He rubbed himself to and fro. His nose waved in the air.

"There is nothing better than a good tail-rub," the happy toss of his head seemed to say.

It was a funny sight. At any other time, Oliver and Roxy would have laughed. But this afternoon they couldn't. They were thinking of just one thing. And that was—one, only one, of the big brown cooling pans.

You see, there were nine of them, nine pans of hot sugary syrup slowly cooling in a long, long row. You remember, too, that Roxy and Oliver had planned to eat the sweet scrapings when the pans were emptied.

Here was the trouble.

There were nine pans. That meant four apiece to scrape, and one over.

But who was to have the extra pan?

They sat on the gateposts and argued. There is no telling how many times they said the very same thing.

"It is mine," said Roxy firmly, for the very last time. "That pan belongs to me. All this syrup belongs to my father, every single drop."

"It ought to be mine," retorted Oliver hotly. "I am

company, and you always give company the best."

At this, they turned their backs on one another. They swung round so that Roxy was staring at Old Moody and Oliver was looking down at Beely's rainbow house.

That was why they didn't see Silas squeeze out from under the barn door. Silas felt happy. He was smiling again his little cat smile.

They didn't see him scoot like a streak of lightning straight over to the porch.

Of course, they didn't see him land with all four feet in a pan of syrup! He was going so fast he couldn't have stopped himself if he had tried.

But they did hear Silas's calls for help. They were loud and piercing cries.

"Me-o-ow! Me-o-ow! Me-o-ow!" cried Silas.

Silas was frightened. He was trying to pull his paws from the thick, sticky syrup, and he was finding that he couldn't. No wonder he lifted his voice and cried "Me-e-o-ow!"

It took a moment for Roxy and Oliver to see what had happened. By that time another friend had come to Silas's aid.

It was Calico. He saw Silas in trouble, and this is what he did.

Over to the porch trotted Calico. He looked down at poor Silas with a friendly air. Then he put one hoof on the edge of the pan that kept Silas prisoner. He held it firmly in place.

With this help, Silas tried once more to free himself. The pan was steady now. It did not move with every jerk. One by one, up came each heavy dripping paw. At last Silas found himself back on the porch. He was sticky, he was frightened, but he was safe.

By this time, Oliver and Roxy had reached the porch.

"Perhaps his feet are burned off," cried Roxy excitedly.

She picked up her kitten and ran into the house.

This left Oliver and Calico alone.

"I never knew a pony like you," said the little boy. "You helped your friend. You don't fight with him."

The next moment Oliver was scrubbing Calico's nose with the palm of his hand. He knew Calico liked that. It was meant as a treat.

Back came Roxy.

“Mother is washing Silas’s paws,” said she agreeably. “The syrup wasn’t hot. He isn’t burned at all. And we are not to have another taste of syrup until tomorrow, Mother says.”

Roxy spoke so pleasantly that you wouldn’t think she had ever been cross.

“There isn’t any extra pan now. Silas has spoiled it,” went on Roxy. “But if there was, you could have it.”

“No, it would be yours,” answered Oliver quickly. “I wouldn’t take it away from you for the world.”

Roxy was about to answer this generous speech when something made her stare and call out.

“Look! Look!” cried Roxy, almost stepping into the ninth pan as Silas had done. “See what Calico is doing! Oh, do look!”

Clever little Calico!

He was dancing. On his hind legs in the snow, he turned round and round and round.

Then he stepped backward, backward, backward—and walked into the barn door with a bump!

This made Watch, still shut in the barn, bark joyfully. He thought he was going to be let out.

But the bump brought Calico down to the ground again. He swished his tail with a mischievous air. Then he pawed at a snow-bank and looked thoughtful.

What was he thinking?

Who can tell?

But it may be that he was wondering, “Why don’t they guess my secret? Where do they think I learned my tricks?”

CHAPTER 10
THE GREAT FLOOD

It began to rain on Monday. It was a warm heavy rain that melted the winter's ice and snow. The melted snow ran away in little rivulets. It came trickling down Old Moody along every narrow valley and slope.

Tuesday, Wednesday, and Thursday it was still raining. The mountains were hidden behind thick clouds. The whole world looked dim and foggy and gray.

Oliver and Roxy couldn't think of going to school.

Mr. Hatfield telephoned from town that they must not try.

"The roads are deep mud and slush," he said. "You children and Calico are better off at home."

Mr. Hatfield had gone to town on business. He meant to stay a week or ten days. One of the town churches needed a new roof, and a porch was to be built on the parsonage too.

In this warmer weather, the little brook lost its icy covering. Such a mad, roaring little brook it had grown to be! Day and night you could hear it shouting as it rushed and swirled and foamed along.

The barnyard was a puddle. Mrs. Hatfield and Roxy and Oliver splashed to and fro as they cared for Poky and Calico and the hens.

It was Thursday night after supper that Roxy went down to the cellar for apples.

She came back with her eyes round as buttons.

"The cellar is full of water," announced Roxy. "I couldn't reach the apple barrel, and the tubs and boxes are floating all around."

At this news, Mrs. Hatfield went down to the cellar. She came back looking troubled.

"I wish it would stop raining," said she. "I am afraid that the brook will overflow."

"Beely didn't come home tonight," said Oliver, peering out of the window. "Perhaps he couldn't get here. His house is dark. There isn't a single light."

Louder and louder roared the brook. Harder and harder drummed the rain on the roof.

Crash! Bang! Crash!

Everyone jumped up. You couldn't sit still with such a noise just outside the door. Watch barked loudly. Silas darted under the stove.

"What is it?" called out Roxy in a fright. "Has the roof blown off?"

"It is the barn!" exclaimed Oliver, thinking, first of all, of Calico. "The barn has fallen down."

"It is the bridge," said Mrs. Hatfield. "The brook has swept the bridge away."

Out to the front porch they hurried. Oliver turned on the porch lights. Then you could see all round about the dark night.

Mrs. Hatfield had been right. The shaky little wooden bridge was gone. The strong rushing waters of the brook had torn the boards from their places and sent them dashing downstream.

"There they go! There go the boards! I see them!" shouted Oliver, pointing to the dark, heaving waters.

Perhaps he did see the boards floating away. In the storm, it was hard to tell.

Roxy held fast to her mother in the wind and the rain that beat upon them. She didn't speak. She was looking at the brook that she had known so many years, the pleasant, friendly little brook with its quiet, cheerful song.

Tonight, it did not seem like the same stream of water. Tonight it was a rushing, foaming torrent, fierce and strong. It swept along, carrying with it branches of trees and small bushes and pieces of wood.

More than that, the brook had overflowed its banks as Mrs. Hatfield had feared. The ground about Roxy's house was covered with water. The road was under water too.

"Is it deep? Is it deep?" called Oliver, dipping a cautious toe.

But before he could learn how high the water had risen, out went the lights on the porch.

At the same moment, out went every light in every room in the house.

“The electric wires must be down,” said Mrs. Hatfield, leading the children back into the house. “Stand still until I light a candle.”

By the dim candlelight, Mrs. Hatfield went straight to the telephone.

“You are going to call Father, aren’t you,” asked Roxy, “and tell him what has happened?”

But there was no answer on the telephone.

“The telephone wires are down too,” said Oliver wisely. “We are marooned. I am going to get a stick and measure how deep the water is.”

The water measured four inches on the stick. In an hour it was five inches deep. But it had not yet reached the lowest step of the porch.

Mrs. Hatfield had been busy rolling up rugs and standing chairs on top of the tables.

“Let us hope the water will not rise high enough to come into the house,” she said. “Now we must go to bed. It is after ten o’clock.”

Upstairs they went to bed. Silas and Watch went with them too, without being asked. Silas curled up on the foot of Roxy’s bed. Watch stretched himself in the hall at the head of the stairs.

It was hard to go to sleep. The brook roared.

The rain beat on the roof. If only the heavy, steady drumming of the rain would stop.

But the drumming didn't stop all night long.

In the morning, it was still raining.

When Mrs. Hatfield and Oliver and Roxy looked out, they saw water everywhere. It covered the barnyard, the garden, and the road.

But the water had risen only high enough to reach the lowest step of the porch.

"It is nine inches deep," said Oliver, flourishing his wet measuring stick. "That isn't deep at all."

Mrs. Hatfield shook her head.

"Our house stands on the highest ground in Little Turkey," said she. "Think how deep the water must be around the other houses. I hope everyone is safe."

The foaming brook was still rushing and thundering by. The rain still beat against the windows and on the roof.

But now there was another noise above the sound of the waters.

Thump! Thump! Thump! Bang! Thump!

It was Calico, pounding in his stall. Of course, Calico and Poky and the hens must be fed. Poky must be milked too. Someone must go to the barn.

So Mrs. Hatfield and Oliver started out. Mrs. Hatfield wore Mr. Hatfield's high rubber boots. Oliver had a stick and Mrs. Hatfield a broom to steady them. They held fast to one another. The water rushed downhill toward them. It came to the tops of Oliver's boots. The current was very strong.

Roxy waited for them on the back porch. Never had she seen such a sight. The land under water! Down the road, where the ground was low, the water seemed very deep indeed.

What was that noise? The clang of a bell? Who was ringing it?

And what was this coming slowly toward Roxy's house? It moved along between the fences over what had once been the road.

It was a boat!

"It is Captain Daggett in his rowboat that he keeps in his barn!" exclaimed Roxy out loud, though there was no one but Silas and Watch to hear. "Mrs. Daggett is with him, and Mr. and Mrs. Poole. Mr. Poole's arm is tied up. He must have been hurt. Mother! Mother! Come! Hurry, do!"

Roxy ran up and down the porch in great excitement. She waved her arms and called as loud as she could. Mrs. Hatfield and Oliver, in answer to Roxy's cries, came splashing back to the house.

What was happening seemed too strange to be true.

But it was true.

Captain Daggett rowed slowly along in the old boat that he had kept from his seafaring days. It was so frail and leaky a boat that the water came seeping through the cracks between the boards. Mrs. Daggett and Mrs. Poole were kept busy with saucepans bailing out the water. Mr. Poole couldn't help at all. His wrist was bandaged. His arm was in a sling.

At the foot of Roxy's garden, the ground sloped upward and the water was shallow. Here Captain Daggett tied his boat to the fence.

He helped his passengers step out. Then they came splashing through the water up to the front porch where Mrs. Hatfield and the children stood waiting for them.

"The water is knee-deep on the ground floor of both our houses," began Mrs. Daggett before she reached the steps. "Everything is soaked through and through. But weren't we thankful for Captain Daggett's old boat!"

"Mr. Poole has cut his wrist," called out Mrs. Poole, stepping slowly along, plop, plop, plop. "I don't know how he did it, and no more does he."

"The worst of it is I can't help any," was Mr. Poole's answer as he looked at his bandaged arm.

"That bell you hear ringing," said Captain Daggett from the foot of the steps, "that bell you hear ringing is the Peters calling for help."

"Aunt Eliza Webb has gone over the mountain a-visiting," broke in Mrs. Daggett. "But the Peters have got to be brought up here to high ground, and who is to do it? Captain Daggett's boat is too leaky. It can't make even one more trip."

"We can't leave the Peters to starve and likely drown in the bargain," said Mrs. Poole, very truly. "Their house is so flimsy, the flood could sweep it away. They must be saved, and who is to do it? Mr. Poole can't help a mite."

There they all stood looking at one another.

Ding dong! Ding dong! Ding dong! rang the bell.

"Help! Help! Help!" it seemed to say.

What was to be done? Who would save the Peters?

Suddenly Oliver spoke out.

"I know who will do it," said Oliver. "Calico and I will. You just let us try."

CHAPTER 11

OLIVER RIDES CALICO

This speech of Oliver's took everyone by surprise. How could a little boy and a pony save the Peters family from the flood?

Oliver was eager to tell them. He knew how he could do it. He knew very well.

"Calico and I will ride down to the Peters," began Oliver, "and bring them up here one at a time. Calico can carry two people. We can do it, I know."

"I couldn't think of letting you go," said Mrs. Hatfield firmly. "It would be dangerous. The water is far too deep."

"But Calico can swim," explained Oliver. "Don't you remember the day your father took us down to the river, Roxy? I rode on Calico in the water then."

"Yes, I remember," agreed Roxy. "Calico wasn't one bit afraid of the water, Father said."

"The water isn't deep all the way," went on Oliver. "Calico could walk, and then he could swim. And if I had to, I could swim too. I know how."

"It is about a quarter of a mile down to the Peters," said Captain Daggett. "If I wasn't too heavy to ride the pony, I would go in a minute myself."

"We women might offer," said Mrs. Daggett, "but not one of us can swim."

"Calico and I can do it," repeated Oliver. "I will be careful."

"Hear that bell ringing!" exclaimed Captain Daggett. "Sounds like Doomsday!"

"Frightened to death, they are," added Mrs. Poole tearfully. "Are we going to leave the Peters to drown?"

"It looks as if Oliver is the one to go," said Captain Daggett. "Will you be careful, sonny? If anything went wrong, you could give a big shout, and somehow or other I would come."

So it was settled.

Oliver and Calico were to go and bring back the Peters, one by one.

Before long the little boy and the calico pony had started.

On the porch, they all stood watching.

Calico walked boldly through the water that grew deeper and deeper the farther they went downhill.

Oliver sat firm and straight in the saddle. He held fast to the reins. When the ground gave under Calico's feet and the pony began to swim, Oliver held on tighter than before.

"They are a fine plucky pair," said Mr. Poole heartily.

And you may be sure that everyone who heard him thought so too.

On they went, the black and white pony and the sturdy yellow-haired boy. Now the turn in the road hid them from sight.

Then the people who had come through the flood went indoors to dry their clothes by the fire. But Roxy and her mother kept watch on the porch.

By and by the bell stopped ringing.

"The Peters must see Oliver coming," Roxy said.

How long it seemed until the pony and the little boy came in sight again!

"Here they come! Here they come!" called Roxy.

Sure enough, there they were, bobbing along through the water. The pony's head was strained forward. The boy was talking, cheering the pony on.

"We are almost there, Calico," Roxy heard Oliver say.

But they were not alone. In front of Oliver, wrapped in a red shawl, sat Milly Minerva. She made a round plump bundle. Behind Oliver, peering out and holding tight, was little Jeff.

Up to the porch steps walked Calico with his burden. The water ran down his chest and dripped from his legs. But he lifted his head proudly. There was a wise look in his eyes. He acted as if he understood what was expected of him and meant to do it, too.

"They are the littlest," explained Oliver, as the

MAGINEL WRIGHT BARNEY

children were lifted from the pony's back. "That is why they came first. Milly Minerva is fastened on. So is Jeff. Calico is splendid. He won't be tired for a long time yet."

So that is how Oliver and Calico brought the Peters family to safety. Jeff and Milly Minerva, Hannah, Lucy, Mrs. Peters, Mr. Peters, Calico carried them all.

Five times the staunch little pony traveled through the cold rushing water. Five times he swam and waded back against the current, carrying a double load.

He and Oliver were cold and wet and tired when at last the task was done. But even at that, Oliver could smile at Roxy when he was helped from the pony's back the very last time.

Mrs. Hatfield had been warming blankets before the fire.

Now she stood in the front doorway and spoke.

"Oliver, you are a brave boy," called Mrs. Hatfield. "We are all proud of you! Now you come straight in and have some hot milk and get between warm blankets as fast as ever you can. What a story I shall have to write your father!"

"But it was Calico," returned Oliver, his hand on his wet pony's neck. "We must look after him. Will somebody give him a rubdown and something hot to drink?"

"I will. Let me do it," answered Mr. Peters quickly. "I would be glad to do more than that for the pony that saved us all from the flood."

At this, the Peters children looked at one another.

"Not all!" cried Hannah, with a burst of sobs. "Anna Maria has been swept away to Kingdom Come."

And, turning their backs, the Peters children wept loudly at the fate of the pink and white pig.

"Well, you are a plucky pair," said Captain Daggett, as Oliver gave his pony a parting pat. "You make a fine team. But what will you do, sonny, when your pony is sold? Summer people want to buy him, so Farmer Drake says."

"Sell him?" answered Oliver, turning round in surprise. "Sell Calico, after what he and I did together today? Farmer Drake can't sell him away from me. He is my pony."

The little boy looked after Calico and Mr. Peters, who already were splashing off toward the barn.

"Don't forget Calico's blanket, Mr. Peters," called Oliver. "And couldn't you make him a hot bran mash?"

CHAPTER 12
BRIGHT WEATHER

The next morning the sun was shining. This made the whole world look different in spite of the flood.

Now, with clear weather, little by little the water grew less and less and less. At last, the day came when the ground could be seen once more.

It was a soft, soaking, muddy ground, to be sure. But the spring sun was warm. The spring wind was strong. Between them, they dried the mud so that very soon you could walk about without sinking in and sticking fast.

Then the company went home from Roxy's. They went to clean the mud and dirt out of their houses and dry them in the wind and the sun.

Roxy and Oliver were sorry to have their visitors leave them. They had enjoyed the bustle of company and the excitement of the flood.

"Wasn't it fun to find sleeping places for everybody?" said Roxy, smiling at the thought. "I slept with Lucy and Hannah. I like to sleep three in a bed."

"I am glad we have the telephone and the electric lights again," said Oliver. "It seemed dark, with only oil lamps and candles to burn."

"Do you remember," asked Roxy, "the day Claribel came floating down from the hen house, and I caught her in a dishpan? If I hadn't saved her, how could I earn the money to buy my mother a new gold thimble? I hope we can go to town soon and sell more eggs."

"Wasn't it wonderful that Anna Maria wasn't drowned after all," went on Oliver. "It was clever of her to climb up on the woodpile and stay there. The Peters were sure that she had been swept away and drowned."

"It must have been dreadful for her on the woodpile," said Roxy. "She looks quite thin. But the best thing of all is that Beely can drive around again and has taken your letter. I do hope we have an answer soon."

That very morning, when Beely came driving up to the gate, Oliver had been waiting for him with a letter. He had written it to his father, in England, days before.

Roxy had helped him write it. It was a letter all about Calico.

To begin with, it told about the flood and the brave part Calico had played. It explained what a wonderful pony he was, so wise, so good-tempered, so clever. It told, too, of his three surprising tricks.

Last of all, the letter asked Mr. Pope to buy Calico for Oliver. Farmer Drake, any day now, might sell the pony. Summer folks wanted him. An answer must come soon, Oliver wrote.

"How long must we wait for an answer?" asked Roxy. "It would be dreadful if Calico was sold before we heard."

"It will take two weeks," replied Oliver thoughtfully, "a week for a letter to go and another week to come. I can hardly wait so long. What would I do if Calico was sold away from me? I am going out to the barn to see him. Do you want to come too?"

"Whoo!" said Calico through his nose when he heard Oliver coming.

Thump! Thump! Thump! said his little hoofs, too.

This was by way of friendly greeting. Calico had had his breakfast hours ago.

"Isn't he a rascal?" said Oliver fondly, as Calico blew at him again and lashed out with his tail. "He has the frisks this morning, Roxy. Come out in the yard, Calico. See how you have kicked the straw in your stall."

Calico thumped the floor playfully. He pawed at the tumbled straw. Then he trotted out of the stall.

As he went, his hoof sent something flying. It was something small that rolled swiftly and came to rest against Oliver's foot.

Calico was out in the barnyard.

But Oliver was standing still by the pony's stall. He was looking down, staring at his foot. Suddenly he stooped.

Then he shouted!

"Roxy! Hey, Roxy! Come! Come quick!" he called.

Roxy sped down the stairs from the hayloft where she had been searching for Claribel's eggs.

Oliver met her with outstretched hand.

In his hand lay—the lost gold thimble!

There was no mistaking it. It was dull, to be sure. It had lost its fine glitter. But it was Mrs. Hatfield's birthday thimble. No one need look twice to see that.

"It is!" cried Roxy, holding up the thimble. "See the little gold flowers! It is my mother's beautiful thimble! Who found it? Oh! Oh! My mother's gold thimble isn't lost anymore!"

Roxy was dancing with excitement.

Oliver was excited too. His eyes were wide, and his cheeks were very red.

"Calico found it! Calico found it in his stall and pushed it against my foot," he answered, talking very fast.

"Where was it? Where did he find it?" asked Roxy, bewildered.

"Don't you see what happened, Roxy?" was Oliver's answer. "You did drop the thimble in Calico's stall the day that you lost it. It must have rolled into a crack. And Calico stamped it out this morning. I told you he had the frisks."

"He pushed it over to your foot on purpose," declared Roxy joyfully. "I know he did. He wanted me to find my mother's thimble. I must run and tell Mother that her thimble is found."

But halfway to the barn door, Roxy whirled around.

"Why, Oliver," exclaimed Roxy, "I won't have to buy another thimble, will I? And I have all that money from Claribel's eggs. Just think of the lovely things I can buy!"

"You had better thank Calico," suggested Oliver as he followed Roxy into the yard. "If it weren't for Calico, that thimble would still be down in a crack."

"I know it," agreed Roxy eagerly. "I do want to thank him. Where is he?"

Then she stood still.

“Listen! I hear music,” said Roxy. “Look at Calico down by the gate.”

What was that standing in the road? Calico was looking at it and listening to it, too.

Roxy, holding fast to the thimble, ran down to the gate. Oliver followed close at her heels.

“I know what that is,” called Roxy. “I have seen it before.”

It was the car with the trailer that had stopped at Roxy’s door the morning Oliver first came to Little Turkey.

There were the man and the woman, too, who had gone for water at the brook. Now they were looking in dismay at the broken bridge that had not yet been mended. Well they might, for it meant that they must turn around and go another way.

But from the trailer came the sound of music. That was something new, but it was not hard to understand.

“It is a radio,” said Oliver.

So it was. And the music it sent forth was a happy dancing tune.

This was a morning of surprises, first the thimble, then the trailer, and now—Calico! The man and woman in the car opened their eyes wide at what they saw.

For, in this quiet mountain barnyard, up rose the calico pony on his slender hind legs. Then slowly he danced round and round in time with the bright and merry tune.

Everyone smiled, and Oliver and Roxy looked very, very proud. When the music and the dance had come to an end, the man and the woman clapped their hands loudly.

"Does your pony belong to the circus?" called the driver. "I never saw such a sight anywhere else."

"No, he is my pony," answered Oliver. "My father is going to buy him for me, I hope."

But Roxy quickly asked a question.

"What circus do you mean?" she said.

With a different road to follow, the car and trailer were slowly turning around.

"The circus that is coming to town next week," called back the driver.

There was no time to say more. Already the heavy trailer was rumbling and swaying off down the road.

Roxy was looking at Oliver. Her cheeks were red.

"My egg money!" Roxy was saying. "Claribel's egg money. It will buy tickets to the circus for us all."

Now Roxy was running toward the house.

"Hurry! Run!" called Roxy. "We must tell Mother that Calico has found her thimble! We must tell that we are all going to the circus! Hurry, Oliver! Run!"

CHAPTER 13
A STRANGE SURPRISE

The barn door stood wide open.

Calico's stall was empty.

It was early in the morning. The sun was rising. Old Moody's cloudy nightcap was turning pink. The birds were twittering softly and calling.

It was just like any other spring morning but for this: the barn door stood wide open.

Calico's stall was empty.

Oliver and Roxy stood and stared at the sight.

Roxy was the first to speak.

"Who opened the barn door?" she asked in surprise.

"Where is Calico?" demanded Oliver. "He is gone. Who took him? He didn't open the door himself and run away."

This was very true. But it didn't answer any questions.

No one could answer these questions, it seemed.

Mr. and Mrs. Hatfield couldn't answer them. They both hurried out to the barn when the children ran home and told what had happened. They were as surprised as Roxy and Oliver at what they saw.

"I shut the barn door tight last night," said Mr. Hatfield. "No animal could have opened it. I am sure of that."

"I know I left Calico safe in his stall," insisted Oliver. "Someone has taken him. Where is my pony? Who has taken him away?"

"Moo!" called Poky in a mournful voice that made everyone jump.

Poky must have known what had happened to Calico. But unfortunately she couldn't tell. She could only look over the edge of her stall and ask for her breakfast. And that didn't help at all.

Then Oliver was struck with a dreadful thought.

"Perhaps it was Farmer Drake who took Calico," said Oliver. "Perhaps he has sold him to those summer folks."

Oliver's face was scarlet. He looked ready to cry.

"Never!" said Mr. Hatfield. "Never! Farmer Drake wouldn't play such a trick as that."

"He would ask first if he wanted to take Calico," said Mrs. Hatfield. "Can't we telephone Farmer Drake and tell what has happened and see what he says?"

That seemed simple enough. But indeed it wasn't. The telephone operator reported that Farmer Drake's telephone wires had not been repaired since the bad storms at the time of the flood.

"It is because he lives up on the mountain," she explained. "It is hard to mend the wires up there."

"I will ride up to the farm this morning," said Mr. Hatfield. "But I am sure Farmer Drake doesn't know anything about this."

"Call up everybody in Little Turkey," suggested Roxy, hopping with excitement. "Perhaps someone saw Calico when he went away."

The Peters family had no telephone. But Mrs. Poole was called in from the garden only to wonder and exclaim.

"Oh, dear! What a pity!" said she over and over. "Where can the pony be?"

Mrs. Poole meant kindly, but she couldn't give any help.

With Aunt Eliza Webb, it was different. At the news of Calico's disappearance, she gave a little shriek that came over the wire as clear as a bell.

"There now! It was true! I didn't dream it!" called Aunt Eliza. "I heard that pony go galloping past my house this morning. I'd know his hoof beats anywhere. But it was so early, I couldn't believe my ears."

Aunt Eliza couldn't tell whether Calico was headed over the mountain or toward town. This news was better than nothing. But after all it did not tell them much.

When Captain Daggett heard what had happened, he shouted so loud that everyone in the room could hear.

"Well, I'll be jiggered!" roared the Captain. "The pony has been stolen. You had better tell the sheriff and let him get to work."

Next the children ran over to tell Beely.

"Report it to Sheriff Bly," was Beely's advice. "He is a fine man. He will find the pony, if anyone can."

After breakfast, Mr. Hatfield drove up Old Moody to the pony farm.

Farmer Drake hadn't seen or heard of Calico.

"Gone, is he?" said the farmer, looking sober. "Well, we shall have to find him. Let's start out."

He seated himself in Mrs. Jingle beside Mr. Hatfield. Together they rode up and down the country roads. They stopped at every house, asking for news of the missing black and white calico pony.

But Aunt Eliza Webb, back in Little Turkey, was the only one who had heard even the beat of the pony's hooves.

So Mr. Hatfield and Farmer Drake drove to town to tell the sheriff what had happened.

"I hope Sheriff Bly catches the fellow who took that pony," said Farmer Drake more than once. "I hate to lose Calico. I could sell him twice over. Those summer folks have been after him again."

"With so many people on the lookout, we ought to find him," said Mr. Hatfield.

He said this again to Oliver and Roxy when they

came running to meet him that night.

"That is all the news I have for you. Everyone in the neighborhood is on the lookout," he said.

He said that at the end of the first day of Calico's disappearance.

But at the end of the second day, there was not a word more to tell.

In the morning, Sheriff Bly had come driving up to Roxy's house. He walked all around the barn and the barnyard and asked many questions. He looked so wise and brave and kindly that Oliver felt sure he would soon find Calico.

But the second day ended, and no one had heard of the missing pony. No one had caught a glimpse of him. There was not a word of news.

Oliver felt so downcast that Roxy tried to cheer him. But it was hard work.

"I don't see how I can go to the circus if we don't find Calico," said Oliver sadly. "To think that my pony is gone for good!"

"I said that about Mother's gold thimble," Roxy reminded him, "and the thimble came back. So will Calico. You wait and see."

"It was Calico that found the thimble," replied Oliver. "If somebody wasn't keeping him, he would come straight home to me."

The third day without Calico was the longest. Oliver felt that it would never come to an end. He missed his pony more than he could say.

It was evening now, almost supper time. Roxy was playing in back of the house with Watch and Silas. Oliver sat on the front porch alone.

"I never forgot to feed Calico, not once," the little boy was thinking. "I always kept his coat smooth and shiny too. He misses me, I know. I hope he won't show any of his tricks to the fellow who took him. I hope he won't show even a single one."

Lippety-clippety! Lippety-clippety!

The sound came ringing down the quiet country road.

Lippety-clippety! Lippety-clippety!

Oliver sprang to his feet. It couldn't be a mistake.

But there were other noises too. A rattling and a jingling, a steady beating on the ground.

Now the sound was so loud that Roxy heard it. She came running as fast as she could. Mr. and Mrs. Hatfield stood in the doorway.

Down the road they came trotting, three horses, a man, and a boy.

The man was burly Farmer Drake. He came jogging along on Jemima, his big brown mare. Beside him, astride the gray horse, Graceful, rode a boy with a freckled nose.

Oliver gave them one look, no more. For his eyes were fixed upon a black and white pony that trotted swiftly along at the freckled boy's side.

"Calico! Calico!" called Oliver.

Already he was running down the road.

The horses came to a standstill.

Now Oliver's arms were about Calico's neck, and his face was hidden in Calico's mane.

Farmer Drake dismounted. The boy with the freckles slid down too.

They were all there now, at the roadside, Mr. and Mrs. Hatfield and Roxy, the ginger kitten peering from the bushes, and Watch.

"This is my grandson Billy," said Farmer Drake.

He didn't call him "harum-scarum Billy," but you remember that was his name.

"Speak up, Billy," said the Farmer shortly. "Tell them all just what you did."

"Well," began Billy, not looking at anyone, "I heard that Grandpa was going to sell my pony Calico."

"My pony," interrupted Oliver, lifting his head for a moment and then hiding it again in Calico's soft mane.

"So I came here early in the morning. A man gave me a lift in his car. And I took Calico home with me," went on Billy. "I couldn't tell Grandpa about it because his telephone wires were down. And I didn't tell anyone here because I knew there would be a fuss."

"There was quite a fuss after you took him," said Mr. Hatfield quietly. "Did your grandfather tell you that the sheriff is looking for the pony? Did he tell you how badly this little boy felt when his pony was gone?"

Billy looked sober and tried to dig a hole in the road with his toe.

"Yes, he told me," was Billy's answer. "I am sorry. I didn't think of that. But I telephoned Grandpa as soon as his wires were mended. And I have brought the pony back to the little boy. I don't want a pony anymore. I am going to ride this big horse, Graceful. I am going to call him 'mine.'"

As he talked, "harum-scarum Billy's" face grew brighter. No great harm had been done, he thought. Hadn't he brought back the pony to the little boy? And he himself was riding the horse that he wanted.

But his face fell again when he heard what his

grandfather was saying.

"Time to start, Billy," said the Farmer. "We are going to town now to see the sheriff. I will let you tell him what happened. I don't know what he will say to you when he hears what you did."

Oliver didn't wait to hear Billy's answer.

He took Calico's bridle.

"Come on, Calico," he said. "Your stall is ready. I cleaned it for you. You are going to have a good supper tonight, the best you have ever eaten."

In the stable, Oliver put both arms about the pony's neck and hugged him.

"You are glad to be back with me, aren't you, Calico?" said Oliver. "You don't want to be sold to anyone else."

In answer, Calico rubbed his nose against his friend's cheek and nuzzled his neck.

"I wonder what the sheriff will say to that boy," went on Oliver. "I don't mind if you did show him just one of your tricks."

The pony walked into his stall.

He stamped lightly.

"Nay-ay-ay!" said Calico.

He thrust his nose into his feed box. There came a pleasant sound of munching that made Oliver laugh with happiness.

Calico was at home again.

CHAPTER 14

CIRCUS DAY

The circus was in town, and Oliver and Roxy had come to see it. They stood beside Calico and the cart, just outside the great white circus tent.

Mr. and Mrs. Hatfield were with them. In Mr. Hatfield's pocket were tucked four bright pink tickets. They had been bought the very day after Calico came home.

"This is to be my treat," Mr. Hatfield had said. "It is to celebrate Calico's return."

So that left Claribel's egg money still to be spent.

"I shall buy a green collar for Silas," said Roxy, "with a little silver bell."

It was while they were all standing near Calico that a man came walking by. He was a circus man. You could tell that at a glance. He wore a tight black coat and high shiny boots. He carried a long white whip in his hand.

At this very moment Calico stamped his foot smartly.

"Whee-ee-ee!" called Calico. "Whee-ee-ee!"

This made the man with the whip turn and look at Calico. He stood still. He fairly stared.

"Why, it is Calico!" exclaimed the man in surprise. "I should know him anywhere. Isn't that pony's name Calico?"

"Yes, it is," answered Oliver, surprised in his turn. "His name is Calico."

The circus man cracked his whip in great excitement.

"I knew it!" he cried. "I knew it the moment I saw him. I trained that pony. I taught him to do three tricks."

"He does know three tricks," spoke up Roxy. "I was the first one in Little Turkey to see him do them too."

Oliver didn't understand how the circus man could know Calico. Mr. and Mrs. Hatfield looked puzzled too.

"How did you come to teach him tricks?" asked Oliver.

The answer almost took his breath away.

"Because he was a circus pony," said the man with the whip.

Oliver and Roxy looked at one another.

A circus pony! Their Calico, a circus pony!

They could hardly believe their ears.

But the man with the whip was telling what had happened.

"He belonged to this circus," he said. "I am the pony trainer here. He was sold to a ranch because of the hard times. Business was poor. But he is a fine pony, and he did his tricks well."

"Whee-ee!" called Calico impatiently.

He was tossing his head and pawing the ground.

"He knows me," said the pony trainer with a smile. "He wants me to notice him."

So he did. When the trainer patted Calico and talked to him, the excited pony answered with whinnyings and soft nuzzlings and gentle friendly nips.

"You ought to have seen Calico when he was in the circus," said the trainer, patting Calico as he talked. "He always carried a monkey named Fanny on his back in the Grand Parade. She wore a red velvet dress and a cap with a green feather. People often clapped and called out when Calico and Fanny went around the ring."

"Where is Fanny now?" asked Roxy.

What a sight she and Calico must have been!

"She is here in the circus," answered the pony trainer.

Then a thought struck him.

"Why, what is the reason that Calico and Fanny can't march in the Grand Parade today?" he said.

There wasn't any reason. Mr. and Mrs. Hatfield were willing. Roxy and Oliver were delighted at the thought.

So it was settled that Calico was to march in the Grand Parade that very afternoon.

How exciting it all was!

Roxy and Oliver didn't know what to say or think.

Calico, their Calico, was a circus pony! He had belonged to a circus! He was to take part in a circus that very afternoon!

No wonder their heads fairly whirled.

The children helped the pony trainer unharness Calico. With Mr. and Mrs. Hatfield, they followed the trainer and the pony behind the tent where the animal wagons and the cages and the great vans stood.

Calico stepped along quietly. He seemed to feel quite at home. He didn't mind the sudden noises—the roar of a lion, the chatter of the monkeys, the sea lion's bark. The pony trainer talked to him all the while in a low and soothing voice.

"You are going to see an old friend in a moment, Calico," said the trainer. "I wonder if you will remember her and if she will know you."

Now the trainer left Calico for a moment.

Back he came with something small and furry crouched in his arms. The tiny figure was wearing a red velvet dress and a cap with a sweeping green feather. From under the bright cap peered an eager little brown face.

Was it Fanny?

Of course it was.

The two old friends stared for a moment.

Did they remember one another?

Certainly they did.

The glossy black and white pony and the little brown monkey needed only one look.

At sight of Fanny, Calico set up such a whinnying that every horse in the circus heard him and joined in. For more than a minute, you couldn't hear yourself think.

As for Fanny, with a bound she jumped from the pony trainer's arms and landed in her old place on Calico's back. She patted her friend's neck with a little brown paw. She tugged at his mane. This was an old and favorite trick of Fanny's. Then she straightened up and sat waiting, quite ready to begin her ride.

Everyone smiled at this picture. Fanny looked so contented. Calico looked so proud.

The pony trainer was pleased with his charges.

"Now, Fanny," he said to the happy monkey, "let me put a bridle on your friend Calico and fasten you on tight, and we will be off."

This meant that the circus was about to begin. There was just time for Mr. Hatfield to give up the four pink tickets. There was just time to climb to the four seats in a row.

Then the band struck up a lively tune. The red curtains at the end of the tent parted, and the Grand Parade began.

It was a great moment. In the Grand Parade, the entire circus was to march around the edge of the ring.

First walked the trained dogs, decked in bright harness. They led the procession.

Next came the sea lions. They rolled along on low platforms, pushed by the clowns. The wonderful sea lions juggled with balls on their noses as they rode, while the clowns, in their baggy red-and-white suits, made everyone laugh with their merry antics.

Now came the wild animals riding past in their cages. Here were the bears, the lordly lions, the restless tigers. Now and then a great red mouth opened in a wide yawn or a low fierce snarl.

Roxy liked the elephants as they went swinging slowly by.

"Here come the camels," whispered Oliver. "Aren't they fine?"

So they were, harnessed one behind the other. They stepped proudly through the sawdust as though it were desert sand.

"Here are the acrobats—and the jugglers—and the trapeze people," whispered Oliver again and again as group by group went marching by.

Now a long brown nose showed itself between the red curtains.

"The ponies! Here come the ponies!" exclaimed Roxy.

This was the moment for which she and Oliver had been waiting.

Through the curtains, one after another, stepped three ponies. The first was chestnut color, the second was sorrel, the last was black and white.

On the chestnut pony rode a monkey dressed in flaming orange. The sorrel pony carried a rider in royal purple. They both were fine to see. But the last was the best. Calico, with arched neck, and stepping high, bore Fanny, the brightest, the happiest, the proudest monkey of them all.

On they came, pacing slowly. The little riders held the reins firmly. The ponies lifted their heads high.

Oliver and Roxy didn't take their eyes from Calico. Oliver leaned forward. Roxy's hands were pressed together as she watched.

Halfway around the ring, Calico paused. He stood still.

What did this mean? Was he frightened?

Not at all.

Into the center of the great sawdust ring trotted Calico.

The smiling pony trainer stood nearby. He was sure that he knew what Calico meant to do. At the trainer's signal, the Grand Parade stood still.

Up, up on his hind legs rose Calico. Fanny, who knew the trick well, held fast. Then round and round, with neat little steps, turned Calico. He kept time with the music of the band. Round and round and round he turned in a dance.

Then, on his hind legs, back, back, back stepped Calico. There was plenty of room, for the ring was wide.

When he reached the end of the ring, down came Calico. For a moment he stood there. Everyone was leaning forward and watching. Nobody clapped. Nobody stirred. What was the little black and white pony going to do next?

This is what he did.

With a brisk toss of the head, off he started at a gallop. It was his three-legged gallop, his trick. His fourth leg, a front leg, stood out stiff and straight as he ran.

Faster and faster went Calico. Fanny's long green

plume blew out in the breeze.

The pony trainer gave the band a signal. Faster and faster played the music. And faster and faster Calico ran.

It was a sight. The graceful, swift black and white pony! The fearless rider, so tiny and so brave!

On and on they rode.

Faster! Faster! Faster!

Oliver and Roxy, proud beyond words of their pony, couldn't sit quiet a moment more.

"Calico! Calico! Calico!" they cried.

That set everyone to clapping. The people clapped and clapped until it sounded like thunder under the circus roof.

On went Calico!

Did he never mean to stop?

Then a voice called out,

"Bravo, Calico!"

And as the pony galloped round for the very last time, everyone in the tent was shouting and cheering for Calico.

The circus was over. The children were driving toward home.

Roxy had left a bag of peanuts for Fanny. People had praised Calico and petted him. They had crowded around to see him harnessed to his cart.

"The circus was wonderful," said Roxy and Oliver.

"But Calico was the best of all."

As they neared home, Watch ran to meet them. From under the lilac bush, out peered Silas's smiling yellow face.

At the gate waited Mr. and Mrs. Hatfield. Mrs. Jingle, you see, had brought them home in a trice.

Beside them stood Beely. He held an envelope in his hand.

"Here is a cablegram for you, Oliver, from England," called Beely, waving the envelope.

"It is from my father, about Calico," exclaimed Oliver.

And Oliver was right.

This is what the cablegram said:

"Mr. Hatfield will buy pony for you and Roxy."

Did ever a cablegram bring more delightful news?

"I had a cablegram too," said Mr. Hatfield. "I telephoned Farmer Drake, Oliver, and he has sold you the pony. Calico is yours."

"Mine! My own pony!" cried Oliver, jumping from the cart and running to throw his arms about Calico's neck. "Oh, Calico, you are the finest pony in all the whole world!"

Roxy stood on tiptoe to pat Calico's white star.

"When we saw his tricks, why didn't we guess that he was a circus pony?" she asked.

At this Calico gave his head a shake and a toss.

"Whoo!" said Calico. "Whoo!"

It might have been a sneeze, but it sounded exactly like a laugh.

Then Calico lifted his forefoot and stamped on the ground.

Thump! Thump! went Calico. Thump! Thump! Thump!

"He wants his supper," said Oliver, taking Calico's bridle. "No wonder he is hungry. To think he belongs to me! He is our very own pony, Roxy. Come on, Calico. Come on home with Roxy and me."

THE END